Grieve

Stories and Poems about Grief and Loss

Volume 11

Grieve Volume 11
Hunter Writers' Centre
PO BOX 494 The Junction
Newcastle NSW 2300

Email: publishing@hunterwriterscentre.org
Website: www.hunterwriterscentre.org

Grieve: Stories and Poems about Grief and Loss

ISBN 978-0-6453756-7-1

Cover desgin by Keighley Bradford
Cover image by CJO Photography Adobe Stock
Typesetting by Keighey Bradford
2024 Published by Hunter Writers' Centre Inc.

The Grieve Vol. 11 Anthology, is produced primarily on Awabakal country, from work created on this and other Aboriginal and Torres Strait Islander lands.

Hunter Writers' Centre pays our respect to elders, past and present, and extends this respect to all Aboriginal and Torres Strait Islander people.

Some days I feel as though I am learning to walk,
all over again.
— Danielle Sturton

Forward

It is a privilege to present *Grieve Volume 11*, a collection of stories, poems, and reflections that bear witness to the profound, complex, and layered nature of grief. The *Grieve Project* values all voices, from the polished to those simply needing a place to tell their story. It takes courage to share stories of grief and loss, and it is an honour to collate these stories and share them with you.

The works contained within this slim volume are raw and powerful. They are not only a response to death but also a reflection on lost potential, unfulfilled dreams, shelved memories and unrealised futures. They capture the paradox of relationships—with family and loved ones—where care and obligation, love and resentment, are tenuously and inextricably bound. Within these pages lie many forms of grief that are rarely spoken aloud.

Grieve attracts a diversity of voices, offering a platform where underrepresented and marginalised perspectives can be shared. The stories within challenge dominant narratives, broadening our understanding of grief beyond traditional boundaries. This collection reminds us that grief has the power to connect. Each story reflects shared humanity, showing that grief is both universal and deeply personal.

May this collection offer you solace, connection, and a widening compassion for the experience of others.

Katherine McLean
Director, Hunter Writers' Centre

From Judy Johnson
The Grieve Project—Poetry Judge

I feel honoured to have read this year's poetry entries in the *Grieve* competition. I was delighted by the overall quality and often moved, challenged and encouraged by the clarity and resonance the poets managed to weave out of words.

There were many forms of loss dealt with. To name just a few: death of family members, grief for the environment, our mourning for humanity in the cruelties of war.

Reading the best of these poems, and seeing the strength, skill and sensitivity with which they were rendered, recalled a comment made in a Ted talk by an inspirational scientist and human being, Sonia Vallabh, who is on a quest to cure a particularly cruel brain disease that she herself carries the gene mutation for. When considering her fate, instead of grief and helplessness crushing her, it galvanised her into trying to help others who might be struck down in the future. Her comment about her vastly shortened life span and how she chose to spend it has stayed with me and seems appropriate to quote here.

'Perhaps we should live life like poetry and not like prose.'
- Sonia Vallabh

To me that means living urgently, potently, forensically, passionately, deeply, and of service to others, like the best poetry has the power to do.

I congratulate the winners, whose work stood out for its craft and emotional power.Also well done to the poets published in these pages and to those who just missed out because of the anthology's size constraints. To all entrants, please keep sharing your poetry of loss with others as individual grief like all human experiences, though it cannot be known exactly by another, can nevertheless be reached and upheld by the words of someone who has been there.

Acknowledgement of Our Sponsors

The *Grieve Project* exists because of the incredible support of our sponsors. We are deeply grateful to our principal sponsor, the National Association of Loss and Grief NSW (NALAG), whose steadfast partnership has been with us since the beginning. Their belief in this project has helped it grow into a national initiative.

Our heartfelt thanks go to Palliative Care NSW, Pettigrew Family Funerals, All About Grief, Newcastle and Lake Macquarie Memorial Park, Griefline, MindFrame, and the Compassionate Friends. Your support, time, and generosity in judging and providing prizes ensure the *Grieve Project* continues to thrive.

We also honour the contributions made through the In-Memoriam awards. These tributes bring a profoundly personal dimension to the *Grieve Project* and reflect the enduring power of storytelling to honour loved ones.

To all who make the *Grieve Project* possible—thank you.

Awards

The National Association of Loss and Grief (NALAG)
Six Weeks Later — Linda Atkins — Prose

Palliative Care NSW
It Started With a Crimper — Natalie A Vella — Audio

The Pettigrew Family Funerals
For I have loved you — Rita Potente — Poetry

The National Association of Loss and Grief (NALAG)
Shadows and Tall Trees — Morgan Jones— Photograph

The National Association of Loss and Grief (NALAG)
It's All Mental — Natalie Bock— Poetry

All About Grief
Not as much as them — Alex Grantham — Prose

Hunter Writers Centre
Mourning — Damen O'Brien — Poetry

Griefline
Lovely Freyja — J.F. Bolton — Prose

Newcastle Memorial Park
Imagine — Malaika Mfalme — Song

Lake Macquarie Memorial Park
Fever Dream — Sian Taylor — Prose

Everymind
Paper Guitar — KT Major — Prose

The Compassionate Friends
The Water of My Life — Linda Harding — Prose

In Memory of Manny Arcaro
One Of Us — Nat Newman — Prose

Chris Morley Prize for Creative Use of Non-standard Terminology
stone and bone — Luciana Croci — Poetry

In Memory of Yvonne Avery
How to Lose Your Mind — Hannah Power — Prose

In Memory of Robert Miller
The house is haunted (and we can't leave) — Javier Bateman — Poetry

In Memory of Gaetan Briffa
How to: A Pantoum for Grief — Natalie Grant — Poetry

In Memory of Carmela Moretti
Into the Forest — Kate Maxwell — Poetry

In Memory of Antonia Buono
Bruce Dances with His Mother — Maree Reedman — Poetry

Six Weeks Later

Linda Akins

The last hardy survivors; the sprays of orchids colouring the bleached cream of grief have finally withered. Flat dark leaves and thrusting naked skinny stalks; out into the outdoor trash. Squashed down onto last night's uneaten dinner, ants curling up the side of the bin.

The sun is pallid with the thinness of winter and Melinda's breath forms a drifting pale cloud of condensation. Back to the house, she thinks, slippered in the frost. Back to the halls of my loss.

The cards have stayed on the mantle, white images of crosses and doves, scrawled biro messages of love, remorse. We should have known, might have guessed, those cards say. We're sorry. The house is finally empty, holding only the shell Melinda has become and the unquiet ghost of her dead child; head tilted sidelong—thus with the broad white flash of Rachel's teeth, which Melinda had saved for years to fix.

Melinda is relieved to finally be alone. The circus has passed, the mourners have departed, and the newspapers have found other families to harass. Melinda's street is no longer crammed with white station wagons, groomed presenters in grey power suits orating. The bouquets around the letterbox are long gone, too. There is nothing left to see.

Melinda turns on the radio. The police minister is speaking. We have had enough, she is saying. Too many lives lost, families broken. Melinda snorts disdainfully. It's all well and good, she thinks, until it's you. Until it was me—no—until it was her.

Were you aware, the police asked Melinda, over and over, as if sharper instincts then would make any difference now. 'Of course I suspected something,' Melinda had told them, as many times as they asked. 'But I didn't understand how bad it was.' Whatever strange mixture of love and shame which had kept Rachel from confessing exactly what was happening in her house—on that, Melinda could only profess ignorance.

The phone calls, the text messages, the threats—they were only uncovered after Rachel had died. No, Officer, I never knew about those. But it's done. The fires have passed, Officer, and what you see here is only what has been left.

Rachel's room—Melinda likes to sit on her daughter's old bed, on the patched quilt of her childhood and now that everyone has gone, there is nobody to accuse her of being morbid. Melinda isn't, but reclining in this vacant room brings her closer to Rachel's ghost and together they rest companionably with their shared memories. Rachel the gap-toothed child, the teen flicking her long hair, the daughter with shadows behind her eyes on the last time Melinda saw her. Noticed but alas, not discussed. The man Rachel had loved, the sleeping beast beneath his sternum.

The family liaison officer will be visiting soon. She will tell Melinda that this too, shall pass. But here's the secret—six weeks, six years, sixty dead women.

This thing is staying right here.

For I Have Loved You

Rita Potente

You lay bare before my eyes
for the cold winds of death
have torn

the bonds between us.

Love sustained me during your pain
Sorrow filled my heart and soul

I cried as your breath
turned to a whisper
and your heartbeat a murmur.

The winds have brushed past your body
your soul has drifted
and
you lay bare before my eyes.

Memories of laughter
and joy for life
are buried
deep
in my distress.
I suffer the dark, bleak burden
wrapped around my heart
and
agony in my soul.

***

Yet, with time I know
the warmth of the sun will
    embrace me
the stir of the breeze will
    stroke my cheeks
the scent of flowers will
    fill my heart.
You will be here with me for
you have never left.
You're in my heart there you will stay
    for I have loved you.

It's All Mental

Natalie Bock

I grew up in the shadow of sadness;
the spectre of schizophrenia poised on the periphery.
My diagnosis-free mother ever watchful:
'It skips a generation, you know.'

Wondering,
waiting
for that fateful inherited first delusion.
Questioning every action to assure myself of normalcy
before choosing not to comply with societal expectations.
Because my eccentricities are intentional,
anchored in clarity,
not flights of fevered fancy
that accuse innocent others.

There are no whispering demons here.
No party line of spying others
listening in on conversations.
No messages in TV announcements
other than ones intentionally sent.

There will be no brutal electric shock therapy sessions here,
no hiding away of affected family
in institutions as full of stigma as patients.
I am quite sane—at least not schizophrenic.

But the ghost of perpetual assessment remains,
and the enduring sadness of separated family
traumatised by living alongside disease,
coupled with the actions of an uneducated system
that knew only how to inject hurt to heal.

Maternal certification and confinement
forcing a trio of siblings to grow up too early,
the fourteen-year-old now mother to the babies,
and a future generation to be made ready too soon
in case history repeated itself.

The whispers did not come for me,
but their impact echoes loudly still.

Not as much as them

Alex Grantham

We drive up the winding ridge away from the hospital and valley that are threatened by the engulfing river. Gutters full of debris make waves as we turn into our street. Water cascades across the road like a fast-moving creek, nothing is solid anymore. At home, Oliver's crib sits in the corner. (Dormant, empty, futile.)

Tangles of cobwebs wrestle in the windowsill. Waterfalls surge down the side of the house. I hear the relentless rattle and tap-tap-tap-tap-tap non-stop. A pounding soundtrack so constant I usually only notice it when I first wake up. In the kitchen, the wind blows through the windows wafting the bubbling soup towards me and stirring my appetite for the first time. It smells like Mum's house would on a rainy day. My sister comes from the hallway as I stir. Thunder booms from the sky then crack, crack, crack. We both jump a little. Scared of more rain.

'You want to donate this for the flood victims, right?' My sister stands in front of me with a box in her hand.

'No. Put it down,' I reach over to grab, hold, snatch but miss and lose my grip of the box of the clothes Oliver never outgrew.

'New mums need these more than you.'

'I need them.' I reach out to her again. I am weak, bent, heavy.

'Honey, you don't need them. I'll get you new ones if you fall pregnant again.' She stares at me. 'I promise. I mean, unfortunately, losing your pregnancy is just a statistic at your age.' She edges towards the door. 'Turn the soup off in forty minutes and come help me at the donation centre.' She flicks her scarf purposefully over her shoulder as she backs away. 'It'll do you good to meet people who have really lost something.'

'I lost something.' I want my mother. I picture her with Oliver, holding hands and sitting with me.

'Yes, but not as much as them.' She heaves the box to her chest like I am a child who doesn't know about the world. 'Not everything is about you, honey.'

'Go away.' I tighten my jaw and wrap my hand around the broom. I sweep into the corner. 'Go save the world.' I bang it against the skirting boards. Loud, violent, aggressive. Her shoes squeak on the damp tiles.

'I'll come back tomorrow,' she says as I keep sweeping. 'And please have a shower.' Her voice trails out with the wind.

Rain blows in through the open window. The whirling curtains will be mouldy by morning. I sweep strokes of wet devastation across the floor. A Wolf Spider lies scrunched up before me (pretending to be dead). I bring the broom down upon it, hard, bang on it like an intervening god. To make it go away. To make the pain stop. Out of nowhere, hundreds of spider babies balloon over the floorboards and scatter for shelter. Distressed. Displaced. Motherless.

Mourning

Damen O'Brien

Man o' war clouds over the bay let down thin needles of antimony,
quicksilver threads. The brush-turkey rummages in its steamy garden,
surveying topology, shoring one end of its mound. The orb spider
near you has been thinking of packing it all in since its moth breakfast,
pulls down scaffolding, unwinds buttresses. Ahead of the wind
change, the Brahminy kite makes a last circle, nonchalantly scooping
a bream from greying waters. On your grandparent's deck, you scroll
through some blog and sigh dramatically, sulkily, unable to name
your feelings. Your holidays are draining out beyond the headlands
and only unimportant things have been exposed. I've been reading
about the ability to mourn: whales do it, against tide or hunger,
elephants famously, making memorials and mausoleums of bones,
dogs crouching on the turned earth of their owner's burial,
becoming cenotaphs and mankind always, wounds never healing.
Then there is you, crossing off the calendar of your childhood,
already regretting unnameable things. Up the road, the neighbour
drags a cover over the car, the mowers make a final pass, the Hills-
Hoisted sheets turn like tacking yachts, seven black-tailed cockatoos
squeal over the sky carrying a prophesy of seven days rain and I
add three kinds of mourning to the list, exclusive to mankind:
grief for something that never happened; for something that
might not happen and for something that hasn't happened yet.
You and I watch the lightning flicker over the ocean like an
erratic heartbeat, ominous and fatal, while the swifts find
their hideaways, the ants their nests and the bees put away

the last of their nectar and every animal that can, except you
and I, make their preparations for the storm which is coming.
They tell me the North Coast will be unrecognisable in fifty years,
inundated by a rising ocean, that storms like this chip away
at the edges, bringing the date forward and there'll be increasingly
common and savage cyclones. It won't matter, I'll be dead or have
uploaded my brain into a computer and you will be fighting
in a foreign war begun over some pretext or other, but which
is really about the lack of resources, about mourning too soon.

Lovely Freyja

J.F. Bolton

You pick up the phone and dial the number slowly, your fingers hesitating on each digit. The room is dark, save for the pale, cold light of the laptop screen. You are alone in this room. The phone rings for several minutes without anyone picking up, and you start to think you'll just hit the cancel button and be done with it. They must be so busy on a Friday night. You don't want to be a nuisance.

Finally, there is an answer. The voice on the other end is warm and seems non-judgemental. You feel like maybe you can trust this voice. They invite you to tell them what has happened.

You are a first-time caller, and you don't know how any of this works, but you start to speak all at once, the words tumbling out of you in a tangled mess. You tell them about your Lovely Freyja, who gave the best hugs. You speak of her big brown eyes and her sweet nature. When you went to bed, she was fine, and when you woke up, she was not. You sat with the gentle giant's great head nestled in your lap as she took her final breath.

When she was still and at peace, you buried your own head deep into the shaggy fur of her neck and thought that you had failed her. You feel so guilty. It shouldn't have happened, but it did, and now she's gone, just like that. There must've been something you could've done to change things. If only you weren't so useless.

The voice on the other end of the phone has listened patiently to you. They ask you to tell them more about your feelings. What would you like to say to Lovely Freyja? You tell Freyja that she was your best friend, that she was a small island of joy in a sometimes dark and gloomy sea. You tell her you'll miss kicking the soccer ball around the backyard with her, and rolling and wrestling on the ground. You'll miss when she sat on you for cuddles because she thought she was still small. You're going to miss walking with her the most. You couldn't leave the house before you met Lovely Freyja. You were just too anxious, but having her there to protect you made you feel safe. You're going to keep going outside and walking to honour her.

For the first time that day, you smile. You realise that you don't feel better, but you do think you can make it through the night. You realise you should go to bed. This awful day needs to come to an end.

You thank the kind voice on the other end of the phone for listening to you. You ask their name, but they're not able to tell you. That's okay. Things will be okay eventually.

Letting out a heavy sigh you didn't know you were holding, you hang up the phone.

Fever Dream

Sian Taylor

I am undone by the Babushka dolls.

Ones you'd have loved, fussed over, been incapable of leaving the store without. You'd have pulled your shoulders up to your ears and rubbed your pretty hands together like a squirrel with a nut, your eyes full of delight, before reaching for them.

The outside doll wears orange, like your favourite chakra (I wish I'd listened more when you talked about those) and is lacquered to a gloss. Inside, smaller ones are nested, protected. Safe.

I reach to touch them because you can't and am horrified all over again that my hands aren't like yours. So delicate and smooth—ageless. Because you never really got to get old, did you? Why are my hands so sinewy, rough? Couldn't you have gifted me softness?

I'm so different to you, but my heart came from yours.

I remember the time I woke, panicked and babbling about the fate I dreamed for myself—drowning with a weight on my back. Your horrified black eyes as you gripped my arm and whispered your own dream from that same night—me falling from a ship and you casting down the anchor in desperate panic, only to watch it sink with me beneath it.

And in a way, you did cause a death in me. Of the part that knew for *certain* bad things only happened to others. There but for the grace…

Until there wasn't any grace but instead cocktails of chemicals and sombre doctors and canes, then wheelchairs, hospice, and then your grave by the water.

I'm so different to you, but my heart came from yours.

I touch my baby's skin and wonder if you met him before he came earthside. If you got to hold him, stroke his cheek, sing the lullabies you used to sing me and that I now sing him in a voice not half as sweet. Did you get to smell him? Touch his button nose? Watch in fascination while his long lashes swept slowly down over chubby cheeks as the lullaby took hold?

He looks like you sometimes, and it steals the breath from my chest.

I think about long-ago school lessons—the way a girl child is born with all her ova. So you carried him when you carried me. Like a Babushka doll.

I'm so different to you, but my heart came from yours.

And I wonder if maybe a heart can regrow? If there is room in its anatomy for three and not two, four and not three. If there's a way you still feel mine when it cries out for yours. When I see a doll. When I dream of water. In moments of delight, or heaviness, or fright—because there is never a time when the prayer 'Mama' is far from my lips. Or now, from my ears.

I'm so different to you, and he's so different to me…

A heart within a heart within a heart.

Paper Guitar

KT Major

The guitar I bring for Feng rustles under my arm, gossamer paper stretched over bamboo bones. Through billowing smoke from a thousand prayer altars, we wend our way to the temple's giant furnace, to burn offerings for the dead.

'Nainai doesn't play instruments,' my cousin scoffs. 'Nainai prefers money, to spend in the afterlife.' Cousin speaks confidently, as she struggles with plastic bags stuffed with joss paper, folded to resemble gold ingots. I don't offer to help.

The heat coalesces as we approach the furnace, fiery talons clawing ten feet up into the humid air. Chanted prayers to Guanyin, Goddess of Mercy, hang in the spaces between.

I watch as the sweaty temple worker tosses the joss paper, plastic bags and all, into the fire. Shrivelled on the ashen heap are skeletons of paper iPhones, laptops, Ferraris, facsimiles of wealth for our ancestors' enjoyment. Why would Nainai know how to use an iPhone? I muse on the antiquated rituals of Qingming and its anachronistic offerings, deeply confusing to my sensibilities, oddly comforting in my nadir of grief. We pick and burn material things for the dead as a transposition of our own desires, our fears of being forgotten, becoming anachronisms in the lives of our descendants.

'Who's that for?' Cousin asks again.

I don't reply. I clutch the guitar closer to my heart.

I have no answers to why the ashes of my friend are housed alongside my grandparents in the temple's urn room. We walk along the narrow aisles, lined with wall-to-ceiling glass cabinets, filled with receptacles encasing the remains of thousands of departed souls. I switch on the light for the correct glass shelf. Only seconds to find Nainai and Yeye's urns, their black-and-white portraits printed on yellow porcelain, with dates of life and death inscribed in Chinese brushstrokes. They died before I was born. I can't touch the urns in their glass enclosures, so I contemplate their remains in reverential silence. Then the light above their urns goes out.

I leave them to find Feng, to show him the guitar, its painted veneer hiding its hollow body. His portrait smiles back at me. The ink on Feng's urn is fresh.

I grapple with the fact that burning a replica of his favourite instrument may ultimately mean nothing, like ephemeral sunlight on Feng's face on the day he took his life. That some answers, like the extent of the black depths lingering beneath Feng's grin, may never be knowable. The answers lie with those who have died, who are returned to the earth, the sea, blown far and wide in the wind, or who rest on a glass shelf, illuminated for only thirty seconds at a time before they return to darkness and await the next person who remembers.

It is time. I hand the delicate guitar to the worker, who lobs it unceremoniously into the inferno.

With a burst of light, the guitar lasts only a second before it is consumed.

The Water of My Life

Linda Harding

A swimming lesson. I am 5, my teacher an Olympian, the water is her breath, the pool her home. She holds my head underwater because my fear is holding her up. Irritated with my caution she pushes down and says, 'Blow bubbles'. I try. The fear is overwhelming. I push hard against her hand and surface gasping, howling, desperate. I emerge no longer just afraid but traumatised and terrified. I do not enter the water again for years except to paddle at the edge.

I am an adult, a mother. I am back in the water with my children, enjoying the champagne exhilaration of jumping through the breakers, delighting in my children's laughter, drunk on the wine of love and waves. Until that day, when eyes are not on them, and my little son is pulled out to sea in a rip. He enters alive. He is pulled out blue, bloated, barely there. The next day he is gone, and we are immersed, plunged into an ocean of grief, a boundless sea of pain. I am baptised into perseverance despite the endless ache.

It is 2006, the Boxing Day tsunami has poured agony into Sri Lanka. The images of drowned children sear my soul. I answer a call to go with the grief counsellors to bring aid. I am saturated with anxiety, but I go. The villages are devastated. We ride past the barbed wire fences of a land already half destroyed by civil war. I hear the stories of the people, the terrifying force of the wave, the losses, the continuing nightmares, the screams they cannot forget.

In a village in the North, I look high into the trees and see photo frames, books, clothing, a pair of shoes, cast among the branches, the detritus of ordinary lives no longer being lived. Boats sit four kilometres inland, the people no longer fish for fear they will eat something that ate someone they knew, or worse still, loved. This water does not cleanse, it is a foul destroyer of lives. When I arrive home, I have my first flashback to the day I lost my son, back onto the beach in that moment. The tsunami has engulfed my fragile psyche. It baptises me into years of therapy; a 'severe mercy'. I choose to fight the flood.

I am retired, near the sea, the sound of the breakers so close they might lap at my door one night. I walk to the beach each morning, my towel in hand, my aging legs no longer reluctant to go. I walk across the sand, feel the grit of shell between my toes, and plunge into the cold, deep ocean. I feel my body tingle with the icy water, I inhale deep and fast with shock, and I remember. I remember I am alive, still here in the current of my life, still breathing, a survivor. I am baptised into a present and surprising joy.

One Of Us

Nat Newman

I keep forgetting which one of us is dead.

I was telling the story of the road trip north, the one with me and you and Shoulders and Scruffy, the one where the police checked to see if we were okay cos we were two young girls camping with two young guys.

As I told the story, I lost track of myself.

The words came out of my mouth, but in my thoughts I knew only that one of us was dead now.

But who was dead?

Was it Shoulders, long and lean, with no shoulders at all?

Was it Scruffy, who might have swallowed his tongue as easily as he swallowed his vowels?

Was it me who had died, and had I forgotten and been late to my own funeral?

No.

It came back to me.

I came back to myself.

It was you who had died.

I am alive and you are dead.

Scruffy is alive and you are dead.

Shoulders is alive and you are dead.

They asked us, those cops: Are you having a good night? And after we all said, yes, they looked at you and me, the girls specifically, and they asked us again: How's your night?

I knew why they were asking us, and I loved them for it. I still love them for it and tell this story often. We were safe there, we knew we were, and we smiled and told them so (gods, you had a great smile), and they left us by the old train tracks where we had camped.

That's the story I tell, about the goodness of the cops that night. And when I tell it, I know someone is missing now. And while I tell it, I can't remember who that is.

One of us is dead.

Is it Shoulders, who I have never laid eyes on again since that trip 20 years ago?

Is it Scruffy, who is married now, with two half-French sons and a pub in the bush?

Is it you, who jumped off a cliff and slammed into the sea?

Or is it me, who cannot remember which of us is dead?

Stone and Bone

Luciana Croci

I visit your grave
when I need you,
I call for you in my mind.

What is left of you
inside a cedar box enclosed
in a red granite sarcophagus

but the arch of your skull,
a Greek helmet on cheekbone ledges.
edged by your chin's diagonals.
A crucifix of vertebrae and scapula
resting on a pelvis plinth,
your phalanges stiff and pointed.

You, long-departed, dwell inside me
a little while longer.
I am no Hamlet you are not Yorick,
no speeches of pity or regret,
only faded gold letters
white-shitted by a crow.

How to Lose Your Mind

Hannah Power

The word 'dementia' comes from the Latin *demens*—to be out of one's mind.

As far back as we remember, the women in my mother's family have lost their minds before leaving their bodies. I know two things about my maternal great-grandmother: firstly, that she knitted the tea cosy on our kitchen bench; and secondly, that she terrified my mother as a child. She was a sundowner, becoming agitated and aggressive after dark, roaming the house and whispering under her breath. My own grandmother had advanced dementia by the time she died of COVID.

Given the heritability of dementia, my mother and I sometimes joke about one day losing our minds, while privately doing all that we can to hold onto them. Mum has a thousand-day streak on Duolingo and solves a cryptic crossword every Saturday. She takes care of her health and her friendships, meeting the girls for gym and coffee twice a week. I do my best to follow her example, while silently hoping for a cure by the time I'm an old woman.

My family's tendency towards dementia is coupled with a tradition of intense privacy. It has its roots in religion: my great-grandmother was an Irish Catholic, who believed in the sanctity of the unsaid, a credence she passed on to her children and grandchildren. We don't talk about money, or sex, or politics; I still don't know how my mother voted in last year's referendum. I, too, am a private person by nature, though I dislike this quality in myself.

In Grandma's case, this familial fear of losing face meant her dementia was an unexpected source of joy, wisdom and understanding. After a lifetime of guardedness and propriety, she became charmingly disinhibited. Though it sounds strange to say, I am grateful that she developed dementia, because otherwise, I would never have truly known her.

It started with little things. Grandma was a shopaholic and would squirrel away money in her knicker drawer before forgetting all about it. When she found it again, she was like a kid at Christmas, an excitement I'd never seen in her before. After decades of dieting, she began to indulge her sweet tooth, slurping up plates of ice cream and jelly with previously unimaginable gusto.

Then, later, during an afternoon game of Scrabble, came the big thing. The calm admission that, many years ago, she'd had a child out of wedlock. She was sent to a home for unmarried pregnant mothers in Sydney and forced to give up her baby boy.

That's all we really know. She died before we could find out anymore. And in hindsight, it explains everything about her.

As a young woman, I try to practice the lessons of my grandmother's dementia taught me. To be silly; to be vulnerable. To be open with others about the highs and lows of life. Because your mind isn't something you should keep to yourself—especially when you might lose it one day.

The House is Haunted (and we can't leave)

Javier Bateman

I know the body is a home.
I have shelved my feelings in the attic alongside my grandmother's wedding dress.
My mind is somewhere in the basement—held back with packing tape, gnawed at by vermin.
You are here, deeper still. Somewhere in the foundations,
a smell leaks out.
You are dead in the crawl space and I don't have the guts to pull you out.
But it is December. So, I must be brave again.

You are dead. I can acknowledge that.
But you are nestled so permanently between my rubber band tendons—
perhaps god listened to me
when I begged him to *take me instead.*

The body is a home I am walking through with a sledgehammer.
Rooms full of blood. Rooms full of prayers. Rooms of skin and hair and teeth and nails and
you move my legs, my tongue.

We are knocking out the kitchen backsplash
and the statement wall in that colour you always hated,
ignoring the way bruises flourish with every swing.

The body is a home and I *am tearing this motherfucker down.* God, what I'm trying to say is
I love you
big enough to tear me down and fill the hollows up again.

How to: A Pantoum for Grief

Natalie Grant

Boots on the bitumen; the dog has the lead in her mouth, propelling me forward.
Magpies sing their psalm into the morning, and I try to remember the rules for *groundedness*—
I see the bright flash of lorikeet wings, blindness when stepping from shadows into sunlight;
There: patina shadows on the ochre-coloured fence panels, white picket dreamscapes.

Magpies sing their psalm to the morning, and I try to remember the rules for *groundedness*—
But my heart wants to pull me below the world I'm walking in.
There: patina shadows on the ochre-coloured fence panel, white picket dreamscapes.
Counting in, *hold*, slow breath out. The pressure, heavy on my chest; longing coursing through veins and arteries,

And my heart wants to pull me below the world I'm walking in.
I see the bright flash of lorikeet wings, blindness when stepping from shadows into sunlight;
Counting in, *hold*, slow breath out. The pressure, heavy on my chest; longing coursing through veins and arteries,
Boots on the bitumen; the dog has the lead in her mouth, propelling me forward.

Into the Forest

Kate Maxwell

If you ever want to find my mother
follow the tissues—
those crumpled, hardly damp
thin cotton clouds held to twitching lips
nervous nostrils, spilling from pockets, sleeves
or shaking fingers when she's clutching
a cup of tea or remnants of her dignity.

Like an ancient Gretel
she's still leaving trails
flagging her one-way journey
into deeper woodlands
        losing pieces of herself
        along the darkening path
but signalling the past to light the way.

Sometimes it does.
Sometimes a shred of memory
floats briefly to ground
        a verse of song, a long-lost
        name, remembered tale, tang
of ocean before they're tucked or thrown away.
She's stashed them into cardigans

and creases of her brown recliner chair.
They tail her like tame white mice
nibbling at heels
            fussing about familiar things
            all furred scuttle, whiskered kiss
unintelligible as forgotten secrets
years of unanswered questions.

She must have them close
these soft scrunched papers of the past
            touching, mopping
            all that drips and slips away.

Bruce Dances with His Mother

Maree Reedman

1.

Still handsome and *Dancing in the Dark*,
he strides to the side of the stage and takes

his mother's hand. They grin
and hold each other with their gaze.

She twirls under his arms,
and he hugs her, cradles

her head on his chest.
Once he wrote a song

about her getting ready for work
in the morning. Makeup clinking

against the bathroom sink,
the music of her voice,

and now he's dancing
with her in his sixties.

2.

How I wish I'd waltzed with my mother;
she danced so little in her life.

Plates scraping as she washed our dishes,
faded apron around her waist.

Strappy shoes traded for slippers.
The bare-necked broom of her voice.

I should have,
just once, pulled her hands out of the soapy water

and whirled her around the kitchen
in the golden evening light.

Life Lines

Shona Bridge

Some women are crouched, others kneel on the earth floor.
Their hands move with purpose, rubbing balms
from small bowls onto my chest, pressing poultices into
my abdomen and thighs. Warmth penetrates, reaches
the empty places within.

There is chatter and crooning—
never silence. Occasionally, the women's voices rise as one.
On my face, their fingers paint heavy lines in ochre
and ash—protection for the song that must come.

There are no drums.
There are no men.
Children with sticks play in the dirt.

The women's song starts to shift in urgency.
Their voices leap and tease, a whorl under skin,
urging the hilum of my loss into their hands, held open
like canoes for the crossing.
It is then that one woman lets out
a deep wail of recognition, and all other voices fall silent.

The woman wailing is me.

My voice steadies and finds its own strength. I sing the song
of the life that has died within me, and when my song finishes,
I hear a low hum in the throats of the women around me.
I feel the warmth of their hands,

and I see children,
tracing lines in the dirt.

In Everist's Timber Yard

Tony Lintermans

A forklift is crawling towards my car
with long lengths of merbau decking
ready to load and lash to roof racks
when the phone in my pocket buzzes,
my brother in America, having found
his loved son dead at thirty-two.

The body's a world that wobbles, stops.
The forklift driver is miraculously patient
and helps me lift and stack the weight
of merbau, making the tyres settle
just a little. I pay at the office
and drive away, my seat belt buckled

against radio schmaltz, a pop song
climbing the shaky ladder to my eyes,
cliffs of grief and lava flowing—
can a river ever be brother?
An ocean away from America,
the road home to Westernport Bay

unspools in lowering sun, the windscreen
chipped and patched like our dusty childhood,
shards of memory shared, splintering.
The thought of his wounded boy running
when all the ground has gone, grabbing
for the handrail of tumbling stars

just visible as night thickens the house
and the hidden world steps up
like the horse at our bedroom window
a lifetime ago to scare or console—
there, not there. What can we take
from timber or touch to carry us through?

I leave the merbau unloaded,
enter my kitchen door into the dark unlocked
listening for angels, believable wingbeats
as restless possums rattle the roof tin.

The Different Forms of Grief

Pamela Bansagi

I was fifteen and grieving total change—an unexpected pregnancy from a forced relationship my parents had no idea of because I was afraid of the threats made by this man.

The sudden marriage was arranged and we moved away. Dad and my sister were very much against it. He married me to keep himself out of jail. The first day was the shock of violence. Fourteen months later, living under similar circumstances, our second son was born. The hospital staff did not bring him to me for three days. I fretted. His feet and hands were turned at an angle. He had dislocated hips and his head strained backward. He had to wear a solid back brace and was always in pain. With no support, except for a weekly trip to the hospital by bus and train to check his condition, I grieved daily for this innocent baby.

Sitting by the kitchen fire trying to keep him warm, I sometimes took off his frame to give him a rest from the pain. My husband did not allow the district nurse to come to the house and I was unable to go to her. I took care of our baby using my intuition and love. Once I even said to him that it may be better if he died. This secret stayed with me for approximately thirty years until I learned how stress and grief affects us.

Six months on, I went in with his bottle to feed him. When I picked him up, he felt very cold. I turned on the light and knew it was too late. I tried to revive him anyway. We had no phone. With our baby wrapped tightly in my arms, I ran across the paddock to the neighbours to ask for help to get to the hospital. We went through the process of a long night even though time stood still. There were questions from the police and the doctor … all while our baby lay on a table in the white, cold room next to us. Eventually we were let into the room to say goodbye but were not allowed to hold him. The next time I saw him was his funeral.

Cot Death. I grieved from trying to take care of this little soul. All his pain moved to a deeper, heartbreaking, pain that had no understanding or relief. It felt like I was drowning. There was no support offered or even available. My husband did not allow me to spend time with others. That loneliness was all consuming.

With time, I learned it was best our baby son had passed on and had the chance for peace away from his condition. It depends on each person's belief, but I feel we will come together again when the time is right.

Eyesore

Bethany Cody

Her skin is a canvas of scars reshaped with ink.
Diagnosis gives a name to what's intimately known,
her never-ending grief.
Needle pain is not dissimilar,
reminding her of early morning hours,
cutting new wounds to old words
that bruise the wet flesh of her brain.
A legion of eyes adorns her back
and as she sleeps on her stomach,
the things that draw near in the dark recoil.
Like a Caligo butterfly flashes its eyespots
skin-coloured sclerae and blackwork irises scream,
SHE WILL NOT BE FUCKED WITH.
She is blind. But she has vision.
She sees the judgement,
Things unspoken in passers-by.
I'm glad that's not my life.
They don't understand she can still fuck
and wear makeup, but she can't legally drive.
Their stares and stereotypes just as disabling
As the rods and cones dying inside hazel browns.
But her life is beautiful,
And she is more herself now than she was before.
A collection of unblinking orbs,
fringed with thorn-like cilium,
always adapting,
a sublime eyesore.

Non-Engagement in Lifestyle Activities

Emily Scott

The pathologizing nature of mainstream mental health
Demands that we seek to diagnose a problem within

'Adjustment disorder', they say
As if the loss of loved ones
        Loss of independence
        Loss of an entire home
                Built with love that now grieves
                Built with hands now wrinkled and wise
                Built over years of laying foundations for a future
A future now reduced to a room of one.
With 17 knocks on the door an hour
With 'have you opened your bowels today sir?'

As if all of this,
Reduces us and the depths of our existence
To a phrase in a diagnostic manual

As if the compounding grief that plasters these walls
Is something we're meant to ignore

Invisible to the eyes of staff
Who will later write 'adjustment disorder' on a referral form due to
'non-engagement in lifestyle activities.'

> 'Most days, I sit here and look up to ask my wife what she thinks,
> only to see an empty chair, after 63 years of marriage, she's not here.'

'Adjustment disorder.'

As if there's something normally ordered about the way we live, and the way we grieve.

alive and buried

E.J. McGrorey

in the not knowing, there is a knowing
in the unanswered, comes an answer

under bridges left unbuilt
lies a void that won't be filled

not by time or patience
or soul-breaking dedication

yet you grasp at it all the same
hoping one day it'll say your name

but you know
you know
you know
you know

it's the trying and failing
the flailing and abstaining

the picking yourself up
just to fall back into the same rut

it's the sitting down and bowing out
the shutting off without holding out

it's the long nights and internal fights
a search party taken flight

because you know
you don't know
anything at all

it's the castle in the sky
crumbling before your eyes

the dream weaver that doesn't
the going on that mustn't

it's the retreat and the defeat
the cutting off your own feet

it's staring into broken mirrors
the end of an imagined era

Mango Madness

Bernadette Condren

In 2016, a year before she died, we held a luscious luncheon under the jacaranda trees.

The theme was 'celebration', and the menu was mango.

'When I die,' Gabe proclaimed, 'I want to be planted at the bottom of the garden with a mango seed up my bum.'

So she was.

Not right at the bottom of the garden.

The earth was too hard and compact. Not ideal for mango trees.

Rather, we spent the day before the funeral digging six feet down into loamy, life-giving soil next to the old backyard loo, now home to the mower, the whipper snipper and a fat, lazy carpet python named Road Runner.

We left the seed insertion to the undertakers. They assured us they'd had stranger requests.

Mind. Boggled.

She'd chosen a wicker basket. Bad ass in life. Boho in death.

A lovely young man at City Council chambers helped us with the paperwork. Apparently not a lot of people want to be buried in the back lawn.

We got there in the end. At least, Gabe did.

I stayed in that home—our home—for the rest of my life.

Kept watch over our daughter as she figured out how to deal with the death of her mum.

The years it took her to stop being angry with Gabe. With the world. With me.

'She's dead,' she'd say. 'There's nothing I can do about it. Door closed.'

But it wasn't. Not really. Not when she cried out for her mum in her sleep. Not when I came across her hunched over in the squatter's chair on the verandah, shoulders heaving.

Not at Christmas or Easter or on birthdays when she couldn't get out of the house fast enough or for long enough so she didn't have to be around me.

I never held much hope for that mango seed. Although it was surrounded by the remains of the funniest, wisest, smartest person I have ever known, six feet is a long way down.

And a long way to climb to find the sun.

But it did.

I'd taken Gabe's squatter's chair down to where she was buried the day after the funeral.

As the cicadas girded their loins for another evening of song, it was the perfect spot for a quiet chat and a gin and tonic.

Occasionally Road Runner joined me.

November 2, 2021. There it was, tiny green leaves popping against the chocolate-coloured mulch we'd spread in a circle over the site.

At first I thought it was a weed taking full advantage of the fecund earth.

Our neighbour, a horticulturalist, confirmed it was the first shoots of a mango tree.

'You have got to be kidding me.' I was a bit shocked.

It was a bit shocking. Me and my mango tree.

Blossoming

Brendan Ryan

Although it is an ending it is also a beginning
of loungeroom shrines—his school photos, cameras,
watch and sunglasses. We cry, heave, feign sleep,
remember a life you never stopped noticing.
Reassurance cups of tea, his dog on your bed,
the way a kitchen door jamb has supported you,
a brown vinyl couch—something to fall into.
We talk through the minutes until a numb calm
can be reached. Only hours before he was on the phone.
We resolve to never leave you alone.

Nothing so unexpected as a family call at work.
I caught you on the nature strip—flushed face, unblinking stare
where you sat is where you fell. Nearby
others were hugging by the front fence,
some were huddled in the back seat of the car.
The morning subsided into police procedures, brochures,
the facts we couldn't believe, waiting for the mortuary van,
his broad grin, the Biomed. Ph.D. topic nobody could remember,
the supermarket shelver who helped me find capers, powdered cinnamon.
He was the son you took to rock pools, kept a spare bedroom
at your house for, his were the phone calls you lived your life through.

What ceremony fits a suicide?
Rows of the young standing up the back, a make-shift crowd
of borrowed suits, mullets, coloured dresses
a crowd thrown together looking for a place.
Outside, we hugged, stood in clusters, some of us smoking
behind sunglasses, resting hands on shoulders, around waists,
each of us turning up. For this is what rituals compel us to do
before we make plans for a drink, arrange lifts,
they help us feel certain of the next few hours.
This is how you live these days, by the hour,
grief rolling toward you in waves. Together we watched
you walk behind the hearse, leaving us
in your wake with the questions, his name
on everybody's lips, blossoming into memory.

Walk

Danielle Sturton

Some days I feel as though I am learning to walk,
all over again.

One foot in front of the other.
My toes press into the ground.
As if telling me—*ah yes, this is how we do it.*

And then I remember you've died, and I lose my balance.

It's like I've never walked before.

The Man in the Mirror

Robin Archbold

The day he died was the day you got promoted to the 'next to die' generation. Sometimes succession sucks.

You have to 'say a few words' today, but everyone—yourself included—expects more from the successful writer you've become. And you're inclined to overthink things because you can. Once you've had your own kids, your understanding of the parent-child dynamic gets flipped—the small things that matter so much to a child are seen as inconsequential by the adult, if seen at all.

You never struck your daughter. Raised your voice occasionally, but never shouted, never lost it. She never had to wonder if her father would be at her school sports day, her dance performance, her graduation, her abortion of a teenage pregnancy.

You're so different, but so similar. Look in the mirror … see his eyes, his nose, his chin. For so long you've disowned the shared fabric despite the genes you can't ignore. You wonder what formed him, what made him what he was. How does this work?

He left your mother for a younger woman as soon as the nest was empty. He told you she never said, 'I love you.' You could have said the same to him before he died, but you didn't because he never listened to anybody. So, you tell your wife and daughter you love them before every parting, just in case.

You were there when he died, your body brimming with unspilled words. You won't be saying them today. Today should be all about silk purses, not sows' ears. Cometh the hour, cometh the lies …

So much ballast. You can feel its weight in the coffin of this heavy-handed man, dragging down the room with its passengers and crew into the darkling truth below.

You preview an opening line you won't use.

'My father was often outstanding in his field, twice because he put the tractor into the river, but usually because my mum had locked him out for a variety of reasons you all know.'

You scour the emotional map of your heart and your memory for the hidden treasure. You can't remember burying anything but maybe he did. You search for the glints that will show you where to dig—the pats on the head, the slaps on the back, but the ones you remember are sharper … heavier … painful.

But no matter. You're the storyteller. You'll think of something.

Look in the mirror. Who looks back? What's missing? What will you say? A tentative knock on the bathroom door …

'Are you there, Dad? They can't start the service without you.'

'In a minute,' you say.

She comes in. Stands behind you. Puts her arms around your waist. Deep brown eyes peer over your shoulder. Her eyes … your eyes … his eyes …

'I love you, Dad,' she says.

The tears come at last.

Him.

You.

Her.

'I love you, too,' you whisper to the man in the mirror.

Three Down

Sue Brennan

While we were preparing for our sister's funeral, writing the eulogy, cleaning out her flat, and dealing with the bureaucracy that comes when somebody dies intestate and doesn't have much money, while we were coming to terms with how we felt about the driver who knocked her down but didn't mean to, who stayed with her while she was trapped under his car, and while we were informing those who needed to be informed, keeping them in the loop, our father died.

He'd been trying to tell us—'My foot is purple, I'm incoherent, what more do you need to know?'—but we were distracted. And when it happened, we looked around, bewildered, sad, and relieved.

'Finally.'

We'd been waiting, some of us praying, for him to go swiftly and peacefully. What was keeping him here, we asked ourselves, stuck in that room, that chair, that bed, catheterised and staring at a TV he didn't seem to understand? We wanted him to stop lingering and go to Mum. We didn't want to visit him anymore in the aged care facility and watch him disappear from us. Parkinson's is a disease of diminishment. Our minds reeled back to our sister, also dead. There wasn't room in our brains to comprehend the two facts at once, but we had to. And we began to believe that Dad, realising his devoted, first-born daughter was gone, gave up. Everyone fell into doing what they did best while they quietly fell apart, or very clearly fell apart, or appeared not to fall apart.

We got the thing done.

Afterwards, my husband and I settled down one evening to watch *Frozen Planet*. We'd been working our way through *Seinfeld*, but I didn't want to laugh; however, there were always light moments—fluffy chicks, babes tottering after their mothers, animals sliding down hills for the apparent fun of it, or crashing into things—and I'm sure I smiled at something. I always want to look away when a seal or penguin gets tossed in the air by a pack of orcas, but Attenborough's narration is compelling: *You've watched the fun stuff*, he seems to imply, *but you've got to see this through to the end because this is life!* The orca, or the wolf, or the bear wins the battle, and the herd, the colony, one member down, has to keep going.

We humans believe there is a natural order of things: parents die of old age; they don't outlive their children. No matter what age we are when they go, we are orphans, and with our parents gone, we are next in line. With my sister, the eldest of six, gone—picked off by some swooping shadow—the barrier between life and death seems perilously fragile. I picture the five of us huddled on a bluff, an icy wind screeching around us. Terrified, we reach out desperately for someone's hand. We are exposed and aware now that it has always been so.

Pause

Robert Knox

In these days of blood tests
and biomarkers, of MRIs, of PETs
and CATs, whether for boobs
or balls, bums or brains,
we sweat on news primed to

pierce a mask. We land upon the
doctor casting her equitable eyes
down a coded page, led by
a wagtail finger, twitching
left to right, like a polygraph

sifting for signs. What if she looks up
portentously and inhales? How then to
do a pause—a pause that defies
measurement by stopwatch
or counting? When he sat in that

room, he felt the pause in his guts
calibrated by a conflation of attachment
and detachment to a life, to a life
he'd been living to that moment
and to a life he'd dreamt for tomorrow.

Once

Allan Padgett

Once, as you were bravely stumbling your way
back to room, bed and further oblivion,
my eyes traced your body as it shuffled in frame
towards the number that meant your room.

You were finer than, or should that be, skinny as,
a very thin stick insect, your brain had made up
its mind to waste away, given these were wasted
days anyway, devolved through the mess

of theft of bodily form and function through Parkinson's,
searing memories of your brutal beginnings grew so
deep and wanton they made waking moments
a further whiplash of torture, of wilful disregard by those

in charge, the authorities. All of them, even as your
closing days began their final march to gone. Nonetheless,
you held your head high, you maintained your sharp
inquiring mind, still knew how to laugh and gabber.

Kept the power of tears, too, they spilled their secrets
on most of these sad, finalising days. Close to
the end I fell so low, as you tearfully stumbled your way
along that white broad corridor, dodging rails and aggression.

I thought and am so deeply ashamed to admit it, I thought,
please just die, it is too much, far too much, too hard, too
sad, to go on living this way. I hate myself for this thinking.
You died not long after, taking your pain and memories

with you. I am left with many thousands of fabulous memories.
I have done my best to bury the rest, but still they rear in the dead
of night as I wonder how and why it had to be this way. Wondering,
too, about why I had to feel this way, I massage my guilt, and weep.

hyperspace mountain

Sarah Sasson

when I was five I sat beside my father in a log raft   on a river
it wasn't a real log, or a real river   we perch in this riddle
we're at a theme park in florida, if that helps.
          there's floating   animatronic creatures   *zip-a-dee-doo-dah* chorus
everything goes dark with no warning   we tilt forward
the log careens down a steep incline into water   a good metaphor really.
my mother and sister wait for us on the side
one of them took a photo   it's 1985   it's a film camera
weeks later we get the cannister developed   my small face, untamed flaxen hair
in low res.
if the camera was better you'd have seen my bared teeth and eyelids retracted.

splash mountain shut when I was in my twenties because the movie it was linked to was racist:
based on a southern plantation farm; the song too: its earliest versions in blackface.

thirteen years after the ride shut my father died, only weeks after they found
metastases all through his brain.
a fast game's a good game he used to say, blowing on the monopoly dice.
my father loved amusement parks, road trips, art and long odds:
        hurtling down steep verges, bicycles, downhill skis.
well, it was fast.

now my son and I slide into the cart and retract the safety bar.
he's older than I was but his hair is the same.
this theme park owns it all: disney, star wars, marvel
        intergalactic spider-rodents.
after he died, my dad's cousin emailed me to say she'd lit a votive candle
                he wasn't a religious man
but I wonder   launched into darkness   inverted   hearing my child scream
        parenthood   a rollercoaster where the track loops back on itself;
our adjacent hands touching on the rail   speeding though holograms   if
        maybe hyperspace mountain could be   a kind of corkscrew   the impression
of a prayer.

Angel

Angel

I was born just after midnight. By breakfast time, both my parents had kissed me goodbye, never to be seen again.

The universe was my companion as I grew up. I always felt loved and didn't need to attach that to any one person. I dreamt that every lost child could feel this way.

I dreamt of being part of a family. This dream came true with a wonderful collection of children, of all abilities from around the world. I dreamt of everyone knowing that they were born to be somebody special.

I dreamt of kindness in my life and the universe gave me a beautiful man who also cared for all people. We had little but to us we had everything. We felt blessed.

My man was diagnosed with early onset dementia in his forties and so, with virtually no education, I needed to become the breadwinner. It happened and we lived well and were blissfully happy—accepting of all that life offered us.

As a child I had dreamt of having someone to care for. My wish had been granted.

I was never truly at ease in the corporate world. It caused me to worry and stress about restructures, mortgages and juggling responsibilities. I felt trapped and frightened for the first time in my life. I asked the universe to show me the way.

It wasn't quite what I expected! I became very ill and was left unable to walk. At first, I let the corporate mindset take over. How could I fix this and how much would it cost. I had much to learn.

I gained acceptance. I gave thanks, and even more thanks for all that I now had, including my lack of mobility. I was back again as a dreamy child of the universe.

Life was blissful and others were attracted to us as if we had some magic secret.

Then, the universe sent us some additional blessings.

My darling husband became seriously ill and the universe gave me the power to care for him, at home, until his death.

The little unwanted child of the universe came back to me—to love and care for me and to show me how to love and care for myself. I had all that I had ever dreamt of and was surrounded by boundless love and infinite possibilities.

I was humbled to receive an Order of Australia and I realised that accomplishment is achieving things that really matter, and that everyone is truly born to be somebody special.

Anaphora

Susan Fealy

Grief is like a pair of socks,
enveloping,
a second skin.
Your feet can keep
the socks together.
Step, step, step.
Dress them in hard leather.

Grief is like a pair of socks.
Come day's end,
wear marks
fragile in the weft
reveal one pair
to be the same
as all the others.

Grief is like a pair of socks,
very often black.
Sometimes dove-grey
it can tip the toes as if
pointing somewhere
beyond
a yawning night.

Grief is like a pair of socks.
Take them off.
Place one inside
the other. Hold them
between your palms—
confront your orphaned feet.

How similar fingers are to toes.
How similar hands to feet.
How similar love to grief.

Love's End

Barbara Kamler

WE'RE CAUGHT off guard again and grieve the loss
    of distant friends whose names we barely knew.
They're falling fast and loudly on earth's floor,
    Intoning now, just wait, this comes to you.
Tonight I rise in sleepless fright from bed—
    My husband says perhaps don't write of death.
He folds his wings, no wish to fly away—
    nor me from him—this chrysalis we've made

from love. But we play on, no script for how
    or where and when our late-love days will end.
The tea we share can't still the grief we cannot
    speak—at someday never lying side

by side again. We walk through cracks of light
at dusk and sing each dawn—a threnody.

time capsule

Yvonne Patterson

finely inked threads   overlay cities, highways, alpine passes
Google Maps' satellite view   delineates routes, boundaries
its blue teardrop   pinpoints position

once I saw directions to numerous towns named Poggio in Italy
you'd think there'd be more variety   later I learnt it meant 'hill'
translation threatened my blueprint

navy shadows edge out from coastlines   Maps' frozen oceans
obscure submerged terrain, chasms
deeper than alpine peaks   'here be dragons'

weathered sky-blue boards held my brother's home   when he lived there   paint leftover from mum's place
just before dad passed   mum always said   'passed'

what precisely had been passed?   had they   passed the exit home, lost
their positions on the map   were road signs updated in unfamiliar text
were they simply misdirected?

curious how the man   and years later   the son, passed
the turnoff home   at exactly the same age   a shared map
coded in their DNA?   'passed'

not that other word, the one with no direction home—
'software update available'   accept, or
keep memory's map   where time's punctuation   suspends

Anniversary

Anthony Mills

This time of year, air full of ghosts
and strewn ashes, I think of my younger
brother Peter, almost ten years dead.

Tidal tug of childhood memory,
its deep currents, waves wash,
rise and fall in a moment.

Asleep in each other's restless sleep,
your troubling croup,
my fear, a blanket of shadows.

In the middle of night,
mother's song whispered
over the softness of your hair,

her quiet face big enough to hold sky.
Outside the stars fly by,
Silky Oak's pulse talking to night,

its treehouse woven into darkness.
Your afternoon play whirled in wind,
on the verge of happiness

that never quite broke through.
Your many-angled thought restless,
mouth with faltering speech

always naming, tree, bird, rock.
Easily teased and quick tempered,
I was less protector, more harrier.

You rise in me as someone begins a song.
The puzzled looks of my two small dogs
when I say your name out loud.

How To Turn Shadows Into Gifts

Izabella Risteski

In the New Testament I wrote—the one where we're still in love,
time dies right here; where you kiss me and tell me to shut up,
because I'm spilling nothing words just to fill up the air between,
because we both know what dying feels like,
and tonight is the night I put everything on red and still I land on green.

There are good ideas and bad ideas, and here we are flirting with the macabre.
You cried and I thought it was for love, but it was like cutting up onions to you.
We re-fed scraps to each other by hand, breaking what little we could find in half.
No longer wanting these leftovers, I came to you here to starve.

There's a blackout tonight all over the town,
your eyes gleam torchlit through a haze, like you've been swimming in jaundice for too long.
You probably don't remember how the nurses kept you under the light on the maternity floor?
Yet, you still want to drink all the poison
and tell everyone, 'it makes me better than I was before'.

Let’s stop this, you and I. Let’s stop splitting down the middle and getting under the sheets.
We’re up next for the sacrifice, we’re waiting to hear a zap and then an ‘ALL CLEAR!’

I’m changing channels on a wooden console.
I don’t know why they left me the remote down here. A basement stares at me,
torn out cassette tape glistens serpently, spun over my arms and a wooden chair.
I thought this is why we tried to get our belts so black, to stop things like this from happening.

Tell them how we ran out of love, so we invented games that neither one of us could win.
Why does that make me feel so pointless then? To have no points at all.
That I am not sharp enough to cut you in half.
I can see how all this means nothing to us, now that we know all the answers are temporary,
that the sky was playing tricks on us when it left for dark and swallowed all the light.

I break my arm and you try to tell me that it’s in fashion now to wear slings.
So I ask you to break yours and you laugh so hard I hear
the stems of your spine crack like radio static, out of tune, over every word I speak.
You’re in that chair forever now, asking where I last put the remote.

You realise two things and two things only;
worrying when someone will leave you,
is rather pointless when their presence already feels so lonely.
And far worse than that, you were clinging to snake skin all along, the façade is finally shed.
As he slithers out of your reach and into the shallows, you thought you were so close to him,
yet you had only ever kissed his shadows

The Rainbow Lorikeet's Long Fall

Renee Pettitt-Schipp

Because the plastic bags and flashing wine cask were not enough to shoo the lorikeets, my neighbour shot a bird and hung it on a long pole over his ripening loquat tree. It hangs there now, drying in the sun, rainbow feathers fading back to dun.

My neighbour's wife brings our bin in each Wednesday. They gift us whiting, mussels, squid, grapes, lemons and, of course, loquats. They keep an eye on our place. We chat at the letterbox, lingering in afternoon light. We've aged together here; them into ill-health and appointments, us into self-satisfied middle age. There is a peace between us—live and let live. Together we lean down, lift out our letters.

One golden day last summer, I stood by the road watching the whitetails feeding in marris on the verge. Raucous and muscled, they were a feathery riot, an unfolding comedy staged in canopy. My neighbour's wife limped down the drive, joined me in the sun. She told a story from before my time when the whitetails would fly right into their yard cloaking the almond—feathers became foliage, the noise of them rising over rooftops, nuts raining on ground. So they chopped the tree down. She tells me the birds returned for years and I imagine the whitetails calling, wheeling over blank buffalo grass; circling a memory, conjuring ghost-limbs where once they were held.

As I go to shut the blinds tonight, the sky is backlit and apricot, fat with cloud, humming with diffuse last-light. It catches the bags in the loquat tree, glints off the wine cask, its square inflation. The objects dance, luminous, slow and sensuous, folding, holding the day's last rays. The dead bird is all silhouette against yellowing sky, a dark spent flower forever descending, until the earth turns and all colour leaves.

Mengenangmu

Iskandar Nugraha

Berkendara di riak membuih
ombak melawan arus
bergulung pada air deras
Karang membatu pada perahu kecil
pucuk-pucuk casuarina menghunjam tepian
langit memberi rindang dan keriuhan

Ranting berjejal, kurus dan kering
tersungkur patah berserakan
suara-suara meningkahi
bagai tetesan getah

Dalam sepi, rindu terpagut
Mengingkari kelam
bahwa duka masih menyesakkan

*Translation:**

Thinking of you

Riding the foaming waves
fighting against the current
rolling on fast-flowing water
the little boat scrapes against coral rock
casuarinas dig into the banks
the sky casts shade, rains noise

Heaps of dry, brittle
branches fallen flat
scattered and broken
they make sounds, breaking out
like drops of sap

In the silence, gripped by longing
renouncing the darkness
of choking grief

**Translation by Keith Foulcher*

Placing Stones

Magdalena Ball

i.

Three-word story: *carry your heart*
a magpie sings: one for sorrow
carolling, like rain but sound

falling on limestone, tundra grey
exposed to elements
rust at the corners, weathering.

All things decay, even time
fragile as the links between us
keeping the soul down

so when I kneel
soft skin pulsing
smooth pebble in my hand

the sensation in my chest
is not sorrow, but longing,
kinetic energy, heat and sound.

ii.

The city is impersonal today
disconnected.

I blow into my hands, leaning into
the space of mourning

of who I might have been
stones for ancestors

sixteen thousand kilometres
from the arrival point

different side of the grass
living hands scraping the hard edge

of loss, not death, which came
late given all you held

watching for a way
to make those extra days count

wondering then as I do now, against
the backdrop of tidy lawns, faded script

and artificial flowers, who will remain
to tell these granite stories.

At Last

Hei Gou

You take the call in the corridor leading to bathrooms. Nodding your head, you say understood and thank you and it's not unexpected and what can you do, really. You return to your desk and quickly and quietly excuse yourself, mumbling about a personal matter to which you must attend.

You leave in a hurry and sprint to the train, just slipping through as the doors are sealed and the attendant's angry whistle enjoins against boarding. Falling into an empty seat, you clutch your bag to your chest and glance around at the strange mean faces. To your surprise, it is easy to remain composed throughout the half-an-hour journey into the suburbs. Examining your reflection in the scratched glass, you are reminded of a waiter magically gliding to the kitchen bearing a tall and precarious stack of dishes, which seems sure to topple and shatter but somehow never does, leaving you more disappointed than relieved.

Arriving home, you close the door and lock it behind you. Collapsing onto the bed, you dig into blanket and pillow, and you weep and scream and beat the mattress with your fist. You generate sounds you've never heard before, sounds you didn't know you could generate, strained sounds that feel unnatural in your mouth but perfectly natural in your ear, like the sounds produced by an animal. Waves of pain and fear and shame are summoned by thoughts of foreclosed possibilities and avenues of choices that might led to different destinations. You declare that it isn't fair, knowing there isn't any fair or unfair, that notions of justice and fairness and worth don't come into it. You doubt this could happen and construct scenes and timelines and stories to explain. You search online for answers and find none. You make and receive calls in which you don't seem to say anything or hear what is said to you.

You lie on your back, staring at the ceiling and then staring at the blinds and then staring at the floor past the edge of the bed, and you list all the things that need to be done and plans that need to be made. You imagine yourself shaking hands with old friends and speaking to distant relatives and delivering a humorous but heartfelt speech, the words yet to be written but whose very idea is enough to make you weep again; and after weeping until you can't weep anymore and your capacity for sadness and your capacity for speculation and your capacity for planning are all exhausted, in other words, after you've exhausted the capacity for thought or feeling of any kind, including hunger and thirst, which, you realise, you should be feeling, since you haven't eaten or had a drink for more than ten hours, at last, you get out of bed and make your way downstairs and put on *Ant-Man and the Wasp: Quantumania* on Disney+. It seems a stupid and senseless film.

Wedding Anniversary

Maree Reedman

Dad opens the door with no shirt on,
his ribs holding up his chest
like a shoddy tent.
He sees me looking and gets a singlet.
We go outside. He steps out from the walker
and eases himself into a chair, declines
the lamington with cream
that I bought him, for the calories.
We don't talk about Mum, except when I rib him;
he forgot my nephew's birthday. He forgets mine.
She was the sender of cards, the keeper of dates.
She pronounced their wedding anniversary weeks beforehand:
twenty-fourth of January, and the Courthouse
for lunch. They were married in one, too, well, a registry office,
in 1962, married for fifty-two years. He's still married.
Saying goodbye, I hug his thin cage, and try not to think of him
watching TV at night after a dinner of toast and pawpaw,
the evening news knocking inside
the hollow bones of his house.

Four-legged loss

PS Cottier

I work the dread so many times
that it's a kind of sudoku in my head —
rehearsing death like an actor a play.
Hopefully one day she will just not get up,
lie too long in her habitual basket
and avoid that dreaded visit to the vet.
There, liquid death is delivered kindly,
but the syringe is always filled with guilt
alongside yellow pentobarbital.
How can a dog understand that love
might write a prescription for death?
She can't. She licks my hand, trust
written in the ageing eyes, so cloudy.
Human minds flick through possibility,
feel the knot of loss before death.
But dogs just are. Until they're not.

Sundays

Tabitha Lean

those nights where the sky was a midnight blue, and the only light came from fiery stars blazing
across an otherwise black canvas,
just before we were to submit to sleep, he would tell me stories as my head lay upon his chest,
rising and falling with his every breath, the soft beat of his heart reminding me of all his travelling lifeblood—his vitality.
the stories he would tell weren't elaborate or fancy, they weren't grand or silly, they had no clever
plot twists, they were just little glimpses into our future
small promises of yet-to-comes.
my favourite story of all his stories was about Sundays.
Sunday mornings, he would say, were reserved for rest, my rest.
he would tell me that when the baby cried, he would fetch him, swaddled, warm and squirmy,
he would bring him to me to feed.
he would stroke my hair and smile as if that bed held his whole god-damned world,
and then, just like that, when our son's appetite was satiated he would lift him slowly from my
arms, kiss my forehead, lift the quilt to my chin and walk quietly out of the room while I
surrendered back to the bliss of sleep.

he would take my daughter and our infant son to the beach to walk along the sand with the dog trailing goofily behind,
they'd kick up at the foamy waters and trudge in the wet sand, watching the dog foolishly chase seagulls.
one would be happily collecting shell-shaped souvenirs to share with mama, while the little one gurgled and blinked, cocooned in the warmth of his daddy's sling.
they'd adventure in the cool breezes, toes covered in sand; and after an hour or so my love would bundle my whole life back into the car and come home with breakfast.
we'd sit on the back porch eating warm croissants, sipping hot drinks, reading newspapers, scoffing at politics, despairing at the wars against anything and everything, laughing at his stupid jokes, and watching magpies rest along our back fence.
it would be bliss, he promised, these Sundays that he promised.
the stories of Sundays sit like a small bonfire in the base of my now, dead heart.
its promise draws me in sometimes. it moistens my eyes every time,
and now we have walked empty-armed from that hospital and my love has gone,
i wonder… what happens now to those Sunday dreams,
the promises haunt me,
and I mean,
can you really ever mourn a promise never realised?

It's Time To Go

Tracy Peacock

The cue came with the phone call. *Go today,* her husband said. As the autumn wind blew, I braced myself and headed off.

As I passed the oncologist leaving my friend's hospital room, I searched his face for a sign of the message he'd delivered. I wondered how he danced with death every day.

Since I was here two days ago, I'd revisited the beach that we'd waltzed along every Sunday in summer. *Let's go there again*, I ache to say, but there's chords and tubes anchoring her shrunken body in place.

Sitting down next to her bed, I push aside the tray with the abandoned thin soup, remembering the creamy risotto she devoured the last time we ate together at her favourite Italian restaurant.

We chat about her puppy and kids until her husband arrives. Sensing her need to share the oncologist's latest news, I get up to leave.

But she grips my hand and pulls me close. I'm doing hugs today, she whispers.

I stumble my way down the hospital hallway towards the front doors. Outside, the air is grim and there's rivulets coursing down my cheeks. I resist the urge to run back inside. I want more hugs.

But Still I Grieve

Rhonda White

I wake up every morning and start a new day of my wondrous life. I've climbed metaphoric mountains, done the work, walked the path, conquered the seemingly insurmountable challenges.

You tell me I'm an inspiration, you tell me I'm strong. You tell me that you admire me, that you don't know how I do it.

You see the successes, the triumphs, the 'highlight reel' of my life. You think I'm healed, that I'm impenetrable, that I'm 100% fine.

You see I'm living my best life, finding happiness, love, and significance in the smallest of things.

You see me. You see the girl that never gives up. Who finds joy wherever she can.

I am all of those things. You see me for who I am.

But still I grieve.

I grieve for the moments, now and forever missed.. The opportunities stolen from me, the days that will never come.

I grieve for the life I planned but am not living. I grieve for the memories I don't get to make. I grieve for the things I can no longer share.

I grieve for the connections I once had--in person rather than in spirit. For the reassurance of a touch or simply a hand to hold.

But I live, a full and wonderful life. I put one foot in front of the other, ticking off the tasks that have become part of my survival kit. I live for those who no longer can. I live to help others in similar situations find their way forward too.

You see me and think I have it all together.

But still I grieve.

A Candle

Bette Guy

I sat in the deep hot water. The blood changed from red and runny to violet blobs, like the liver in the butcher's window. I sat, dumbstruck, not believing it was all coming out of me. I was confused. Just fifteen minutes earlier I was being kissed and promised the love of a boy who'd first fondled me, then fingered me and then tried to penetrate me. Totally startled by the sensation I'd tightened every muscle I had down there. He must have ruptured me. My generation was told nothing about sex. I'd expected the soft kisses, the whispering in the ear, the tingling of nipples gently caressed. But not the pain as I was crushed against the moonlit tree. When I screamed he stared at me like I was an alien.

'It hurts. I'm bleeding,' I whispered, as if it was my fault.

'It always hurts the first time,' he announced. 'There's always some blood.'

We looked down at the knickers around my feet, the skirt pushed up and the blood rushing down my legs. He zipped up his jeans. 'It shouldn't be that much. Best get yourself cleaned up.'

He helped me clamber through the window into my room then dashed off. A hot bath was all I could think of. It was midnight. Dark. Silent. Everyone else in the hostel was in bed.

The bath was soiled by years of use. I was soiled. Was this how intercourse was for girls? No wonder mothers never explained it.

The water grew cold. The blobs stopped. I shuffled to my room and sank under the blankets for comfort. The bleeding started again. I sobbed into my pillow.

The door opened. The light came on. Andrea, from the next room, peered down at me. 'Are you alright?'

Relieved at no longer being alone I threw back the bedclothes and she saw the mess that had congealed in the bed. She gasped.

'I'll fetch help.'

She ran off.

Andrea returned with a doctor, whose hair was ruffled, whose eyes were puffy and whose tie was undone. He was quiet and courteous. He said I had to go to hospital.

Then the Hostel Warden stormed in. She wore a blue chenille dressing gown over her nightie. Her scowl bordered upon hatred. She'd been heard to comment that all redheads were sluts.

'You've been a very naughty girl haven't you!'

Had I?

'It's against the law what you've done.'

Was it?

'This has never, ever happened to one of my girls! I shall have to report this.'

The doctor held up his hand. 'There is no need for that.'

I was sent home. The incident was never mentioned. No police came. No counselling was offered. I was sixteen. It was my secret. For over sixty years I grieved for that girl's loss of innocence. Sometimes I would sit in the dark, light a candle and ponder on the very different woman I might have become had I not been blamed and shamed.

Self-Grief and Acceptance of the Soon-to-be

Jeremy Gadd

Knowing I am soon to succumb,
I've never felt so much in love
with life, with what is ordinary;
with what would normally be taken
for granted: the common sight of
bushes bowing before a breeze;
the ambient buzzing of insects
industrially busy in foliage and ferns.
Even the everyday drone of aircraft,
the trundle of trains and traffic have music
and the monotony of daily routines,
gives me an unprecedented high.
Knowing there is nothing to come,
the mundane elates and excites me.

And like an unwatered, shrivelled plant,
a battery running down, a waning moon
or the abating swell of waves on an ebbing tide,

I relentlessly move toward silence while life,
in all its variety, garishness, complexity—
like a lengthy Bayeux tapestry—rolls on.
Should I feel cheated or angry about
interfacing with mortality? Missing out on
futurity? It is like being on a roller-coaster,
knowing the end of the ride will never
be seen, that someone else will enjoy it.
Whether brief or granted reasonable longevity,
how could anyone fail to laud and extol
the gift, the privilege of sentient existence?

> Sea-food chowder by the sea,
> this is all life is meant to be.
> Above, clear, blue, winter sky,
> split by vapour trails up high.
> On such a day, let me die.

Doris

Shona Bridge

Her pink jumper, hand-knitted, is balled at the elbows. The left side of her face droops with paralysis from earlier radiation. Doris is swollen with fluid, there's cancer in both lungs, and no talk of further treatment. We sit at a kitchen table overrun with medications, medical devices and creams meant to soothe the effects of all this.

She doesn't mention:
botched procedures, side effects,
how 'lucky' she is.

Afternoon sun pours through the northern window of her sagging weatherboard. A bush turkey scratches in the tangle of undergrowth out front—more scrub than yard. When I offer to make tea, Doris says she can no longer feel her tongue and chews it when she tries to eat. 'What has to die,' she tells me thickly, 'is the refusal for things to end.'

Moss on weatherboard—
to listen deeply is to
let ourselves be changed.

In the lifetime it takes to move—both Doris and her oxygen tank—from the kitchen table to the couch, there's only shallow whispers of breath, a clock ticking, and a feeling of helplessness I no longer rally against. We sit beside each other—the couch so soft her frailty folds towards me—and we do what we always do. We hold the albums of her life and turn the pages.

It's a tactile thing—
sharing the joys and losses
in late Autumn light.

Drought

Leon Kennedy

Hit me again, after one too many.

You used to take it out on her.
One day she left us,
I could never blame her.
I'd often wonder if she thought about us.

Tell me which plants to water.

Whenever I'd leave Melbourne,
I'd keep an eye out.
Just in case fate would have it.
I'd even check the local papers,
just because—*you never know?*

Highlight every point of friction.

One day in Sydney I saw her name.
Right there—in the Obituaries.

Gears won't grind,
that no longer touch.

This drought's been going on for years,
but in that moment,
I turned to water.

Defining Moments

David Terelinck

the Japanese have a hundred ways
to say snow and rain
yet I yearn for words to name
how a whiff of Old Spice
on a passing stranger
makes me tremble

what is the word for the balance point
between faith and fear
that moment winter sunlight
stutters through venetians
to pool in the hollow ache
of my need for you

we need a word to define
that shock beyond grief
at the coldness of your skin
as I retied the Windsor knot
just the way you liked it

and what is the term for bearing
the unbearable
when I slip into the skin
that you once wore
zipping up your Burberry
plunging my hands into pockets
that once enveloped yours
my feet wallowing
in your gumboots

Scissors

Julia James Burns

I started with her stockings carefully guiding them over her toes so that I didn't pull a thread.

'Have I got the right colour?' I ask my grandmother.

It's a very special day for her and she had asked me to help her dress for it. The colour must be right because we had agreed on the cream linen suit. I look up at her briefly, but she has closed her eyes.

'Just take your time, I'm here,' I tell her.

'And I'm here with you.' I hear her say. I wonder how many times she has helped me dress, held my hand? But it's my time to help her and I want it to be perfect.

I look at her for a moment and see her beauty, her curiosity and energy for life, the fibres that bind the two of us together for we are so alike.

'You know I love you,' I tell her. But she rests her eyes and doesn't answer. She knows I love her.

'I think we've made the perfect choice with the cream linen,' I say, looking at the suit on its hanger. Her slip is harder to manoeuvre. I don't want to stretch her arms over her head any further than I need to. I manage one arm at a time and edge the slip's satin over her hips. My eyes stop momentarily there and I am reminded that this is where the thread began, when I was an egg within my mother, within her womb. She spun the fibres then to fasten us together.

I ease one arm up through the sleeve of her shirt then turn her to bring the other into its sleeve. Then I find each small mother of pearl button and thread it as I look into her beautiful face. She is serene.

'How's that?' I ask her.

Then I gently turn her to get her jacket on and button it and take her string of pearls and latch them together around her neck, behind her thick hair. I dust some powder over her cheeks and a light brush of her favourite lipstick, twist a thin thread of hair back into place at her temple.

She looks perfect and as I hear her agree, she looks at me and gives me a wink. I know I didn't imagine it. As I stand in front of her and smile, I hear her quietly say, 'Thank you.'

'It's my honour,' I whisper back.

She's ready and I know it's finally time. I reach for the thin white ribbon on the table and thread it carefully around a lock of her hair, take the scissors, pause a moment and cut.

'You don't mind, do you?' I ask softly, but know now that she won't answer me. I hold this last, precious piece of her in my hand and stand breathing her in one last time and then allow her to be wheeled away on a thin silver bed.

The Room with Their View

Angela Costi

1

as the shore turns amber into gold
lacing the tide   in out   in out
watching ants dressed as tourists
their view makes her hand reach for his
in a room numbered 714   branded Oceanic
for its disappearing window
in a building with a roof scraping the lowest cloud
cradling hands   looking out
ignoring the other pent up   moody apartments
up   down   up   down   air   glass   mediating
marriage   divorce   death   for now
they are the honeymooners about to walk
on sand
they will dress   take the elevator from forty-one rungs
find a spot for their feet to tease
the sea

2

the view is familiar

so long ago is not the language

of the tide

she was that tiny honeymooner   peeling burnt skin

her eyes dive from glass   plunge into sea

alone   she swims with the miniature whale

sending its song into the white glide of five gulls

above   below   his casket is borne on another swell

funeral black   wipes the mango from the horizon

what is left to watch

3

the light of early stars dwindles in the wake of her bedside lamp

the window casts her   luminous

phosphorescent

she eases her body   carefully   into the cold sheets

the quiet   folds   the silence

Psychopomp

Natalia K Maguire

Two months after you died, I saw you in a dream. You looked healthy again, fur thick and eyes bright, sitting atop the kitchen bench. When you saw me, you meowed louder than I had ever heard, and I replied just as enthusiastically, 'I haven't seen you in *ages!*' having completely forgotten why within the dream.

You rubbed your face against mine with a superhuman strength that knocked me to the ground. As I lay there laughing, I dimly remembered the reason for your absence.

'Oh, right,' I said. 'You live somewhere else now. Is it nice?'

Yes. You were purring loudly, your body warm against my chest. *It's very nice and I am happy.*

'Well, I'm glad you could come back and say hello. It's so good to see you again.'

It's very good to see you too.

When I woke up, I remembered your death. On your last day, you had found the strength to crawl into your beloved garden one last time. As you lay down, a summer storm rolled in overhead. Birds fluttered, thunder rumbled, raindrops fell, and I sat on the ground with you. You didn't notice any of it. I ran my fingers through your tattered fur, feeling every rib underneath, remembering when you used to be plump.

The vet asked, 'Are you ready for me to give her the final medication?'

I nodded. 'She's already gone.'

'No, no, she's still here at the moment.'

'No. She's already gone.'

It felt like a gift to give you this death. No more nausea. No more thirst. No more stress or pain. Just the last step of your care—releasing you from your prison of a body.

We had 16 years together. We watched each other grow up. Now it was my job to gently usher you out of life with the same care and love as I had carried you through it. It felt like an honour to do so.

Afterwards, I brushed your fur and trimmed your claws. I tied a lock of my hair to your paw so you too would have a piece of me to take with you. I wrapped you in one of my scarves (it had always been yours), and I let the vet carry you away.

I'm still learning how to live without you. I still look for you in the corner of every room. My breath still catches when I see black clothes crumpled on the bed because I think it might be you. When the house gets too quiet, I ask, 'Where's Sadie?' Then I remember that my stewardship of you is over. I was your companion for nearly every day of your life, but you could only join me for a portion of mine.

I hope I dream of you again. And I hope that when it's my time to go, you will return the favour and come back to escort me across that threshold.

A Call Unanswered

Catriona Scott

A velvet red poppy falls apart beside another, which opened this morning, with petals the colour of sunset in a desert sky—carnelian, blood orange, ochre and rust—calling to mind dry dusty red country a world away. Sparsely vegetated, it stretches out vast and open, interrupted occasionally by low terracotta rock formations, whispering stories of what has been.

Remembering sitting out there, listening to Pitjantjatjara women speak about their homelands, I find myself still grieving for the opportunity we missed when Australia voted 'no' to a First Nations Voice to Parliament. Wishing I could lie down in a wide river, water the colour of tea, pulsing with life, swirling over me and somehow magically washed this nation clean of the sense of entitlement, vitriol and disrespect revealed by the referendum.

I look out the window wanting, yet again, to say I'm sorry for what us Caucasian mob have done on this country, for what we are doing still. But what good will that do to the countless people who dedicated years and even decades of their lives to working towards the Voice. Or to the well-being of the families and communities they spoke on behalf of.

Reconciliation is a word which has crumbled into dust in my mind under the weight of our political failures, but holding a bright feather gifted by an Aboriginal child, I know it is a word we still need.

After a light rain falls gentle as mist, water drips from vivid green fronds like glass beads falling, breaking. I wander the garden at snail's pace, covering little distance. Taking in flowers and leaves, rocks and moss, the damp smell of soil, the white wings of a moth, the thin black line of a leech.

My body starts to ache with the effort of being outside, where the world is, where I yearn to be through long hours in bed, which stretch into days, then weeks and months, for years now. Salty tears falling for the places this convalescent body cannot take me, I breathe in the sweet spicy scent of blue gums.

The air feels soft on my skin as I do the only work I can, the work of loving this beautiful broken world, where colonisation is not yet a thing of the past, where voices of value and diversity go unheard because far too much power is concentrated in wealthy white hands. The work of gathering up the words with which to bear witness and say, 'not in my name'.

I write in requiem to a possibility long hoped for, a door closed. In requiem to the Australia we might have become had we been willing to listen to a First Nations Voice to Parliament and follow through on what we heard. I think of the heartfelt and eloquent plea the Uluru Statement was, words I thought were too powerful to be ignored.

Overhead, unseen, a black cockatoo utters a conversational creak which goes unanswered in the empty sky.

Early Morning, October 7

Marcelle Freiman

After the first grenade's deafening explosion—
you watch the next one roll across the floor
in the concrete refuge meant to shelter you:

stay close to the entry wall, the space crammed by the rush
of young revellers fleeing inside
from their all-night party turned terror.

When the gunfire stops, you walk out, one of those who can—
on the narrow sliver of light you've been given—
your life miraculous.

In your mind, you tell me, are pictures only yours:
bitter sounds, cries, what you had to climb past
to exit—the ones who did not survive.

Later, you can hear the loud booms—
rockets from the 'Iron Dome' whoosh to the sky—
the small dog trembles on the sofa.

You watch the television. You're shaken, you're whole—
then go outside, as you do each day
to water the garden—

where the aged pomelo tree grows: its heavy fruit
hanging from low branches,
bright yellow discs in a hard breeze.

Pomelo skins are thick and tough—
it takes work and a sharp serrated knife
to cut away the peel, pith and membrane—

inside the fruit, their sweet and bitter gift
might quench the mouth on days
of hot *hamsin* winds from the south.

Dad's Shed

Kirsten Johnston

I didn't see you as you died,
or after, and though the funeral
pulled us, brain-fogged and crying,
into a past-tense love,
to me you're simply in the shed.
You'll come home when you're hungry.

The shed is full of tools for crafting:
saws and planes cared for like children;
hardwood lengths laid in careful stacks;
chisels as sharp as your vinegar on chips
at the beach; and you, bent over
the lathe, pressing steel
to spinning blocks, or rubbing circles
of beeswax into thirsty wood.
The smell of the shavings is warm
and was comforting once.

I leap to tell you things—
I chipped out of the bunker on the eighth;
I sold a painting. I know you'll be proud
and joyful, though I can't remember your laugh.
It's lost in the whirr.

I look for you in deep corners, behind shelving
lined with Vegemite jars of screws and ancient bits.
You must be in the house, in dusty clothes,
eating lunch with Mum.

Happy Birthday, Baby

Paris Rosemont

Eight years old today! My—how you've grown. You're beautiful, with your almond eyes and chestnut curls tied back with a satin ribbon the colour of the apricots I craved, all plump and furry, as you ballooned into a cantaloupe inside me. Today you sit alone in the nursery in your pretty white party frock with the stiff lace trim and sweet *Peter Pan* collar, sipping imaginary tea from an invisible cup—a tiny one, I can tell, from the way you're holding its miniature handle so daintily between your thumb and forefinger. Seated to your left is Mister Jinks, your teddy bear with scruffy snow-white fur, sporting a dapper tweed waistcoat and matching bowtie. A lilac knitted owl shaped like a bloated bowling pin with flightless woollen wings perches to your right. May I join you? Thank you for the posy of forget-me-nots. Of course I didn't forget. I would never. I'm sorry it's just me again. Not many can bear

to sit through tea parties with ghosts.

House Full of Flowers

Rose Van Son

i.m. Mother

The house is full of flowers—
the glass table where they bloom
transparent reflective—
cherry roses mingle with baby breath
white lilies and yellow chrysanthemums,
green fronds. In a clear vase
pom pom geraniums, pink carnations
the tiniest rose buds, lilies and their stamens
clasp the heart in a bow its shadow
cupped between carnation and lily.
A ladybug rides waves on a narrow leaf
the breeze no longer catches its flow.
Dear Mother, oh how we loved you—
the glossy leaf of white orchid, pure petals
the milkiness you carry, skin soft as honey dew.
A glass bowl beside you, fern and white roses
some buds open some about to burst.
Eucalypts steal through the gaps bracken
holds you close, lilies breath-white
have made the long sea journey
ready to open on your arrival
they have not forgotten you
nor will they ever.
Daises shelf the edge, soft greens
musk pink ribbons console us
as you make your way home.

Hands

Shereen Ricupero

A sliver of light falls through a gap in the curtains onto a cup of lukewarm tea on the window ledge, milk congealing around the rim. The brisk cadence of nurses and doctors, and the clatter of the food trolley meld with the gentle hum of patients and their visitors, antiseptic sounds seeping through the edges of the door.

Mechanical beeping punctuates each pause like the touch of a comma, the sound of her breathing mediated by the whispered prayer of the oxygen mask. I gently cup my fingers around the back of her hand. Her veins are prominent and blue, a network of ridges twitching with the tenuous flicker of life. I cradle her disease in my palm, ignoring the slow rot, the white ants, the sands of the hourglass.

My baby rolls languidly in my womb, nestling up against my healthy pink organs, her elbows and knees stretch my body to its limits as she shapes me into the mother she needs. Once I was nestled in my mother's belly and I stretched and shaped her this way too, and one day my baby will be sitting next to me in a hospital bed just like this, wrapping her fingers around mine.

I trace the dip of her lifeline, traversing its path through her mottled skin. I once piled cowrie shells and sand dollars into this hand, salt spray in our hair and sand peppering our skin, seagulls twisting and cawing overhead as the ocean frothed and lapped at our toes. I think of all the times I wound my fingers through hers, oblivious that one day I would see those hands wither and waste.

I fold into the gentleness of her belly, search for her beyond the soft yield of her flesh. I press her hand to the side of my face, the fall of her fingers following the curve of my cheek. She remains still and the tea goes cold. The oxygen whispers, the food trolley clatters, and the machine ticks on.

Dear Me

Kathryn Bennett

Dear . . .

Who am I writing this to?

Most people think that a few years down the track I should be 'back to normal', whatever my normal used to be. They have no idea what type of track that is—how many potholes, muddy patches and wrong turns it has. What they're really saying is that they want me to be the sociable, strong and caring person they used to rely on, not someone who still needs to dip out of social occasions, spend time alone on devastatingly difficult days like birthdays, Christmas, and especially Mother's Day. Unpredictability is now associated with my name. It used to be dependability.

It's as if these changes are transparent to me, not the undermining thieves of my sense of self. I struggle every day to try to overcome the impact, both on myself and others—internal struggles that I never talk about, ones that catch me out and trigger a chain of undermining thoughts. The weight of feeling responsible for letting people down only makes the burden heavier. I am not being selfish, just trying to care for my own needs. I call it 'self-ful', like respectful, to try to bridge that gap.

I don't know who to address my letter to because what I want to say is so important that I want it to be received with understanding. I don't want to hear any platitudes, and certainly not how someone's neighbour's friend coped under similar circumstances. There are no similar circumstances. No one else is me. No one else was her. No one else lived our lives, shared our love, understood each other like we did.

And yet I feel immense sadness whenever I hear of another young person's death. I feel for the mothers. I wonder how they are coping, being supported. It often devastates me to the point where I have to turn away from the news. I find myself comparing our losses, the ages of our dead offspring, any siblings. It's a vortex that sucks me into its internal destruction. Sometimes it leaves me feeling self-righteous, a bizarrely uncomfortable sensation. Mostly it hits the pit of my stomach like when I heard the words on my mobile phone from the doctor that day: *I'm sorry to tell you, your daughter is dead.*

I often write to her, sitting beside her grave, keeping her up to date with what's happening—initially about her funeral, then the court case, now what her friends are doing and the children they are having. I tell her about my garden, my place of solace and the source of the petals I spread on her grave. But I don't share my sadness with her, nor my utter sense of loss without her. I need to keep our relationship wholesome. I don't want to undermine it with the darkness in my soul.

So who do I address this letter to? Who will neither over-react nor dismiss my needs?

Of course.

Dear Me,

. . .

Scientists in Tears

Joo-Inn Chew

It is not normal, and we all know it. The hot autumn where trees hesitate to change colour. The tropical deluges flooding city streets and rural towns. Rivers turned to muddy deltas, spinning floating cars and cow corpses. Howling infernos incinerating millions of animals, leaving a graveyard of ash. Coral bleached to white bone. Island people adrift in rising seas. Scientists in tears.

The shame and silence as we face our children, growing into the world we have shaped for them.

The guilty convenience I feel as my plane takes off. As I avoid the article on climate change in favour of an easy read. As I pretend things are normal when my gut knows they are not. The shame arising as I meet the dark gaze of a wallaby poised at the edge of a bush track. As my heart fills, despite itself, at currawongs and magpies chorusing at nightfall.

All the creatures, the glorious web, the evolutionary dance of millennia, the gifts of air and water and earth, the compassionate curve of earth spinning through space, the perfect balance of gases swaddling our saltwater planet.

Our crime is too heinous to grasp.

I push away the extinctions, the razing of the Amazon, the disappearance of fish in the sea, the oil spills and plastic islands, the rising temperatures. Rage and shame and powerlessness, horror and sadness stalk me. In megalomaniac fantasies I long to wipe my species off the face of the earth we do not deserve. I would sacrifice poetry and music and heart transplants and human love to protect the rest of the earth's community from climate catastrophe. I would be a terrible Old Testament God of wrath and bloody justice.

I hoped we were better than this. That we were not only clever, but wise. That we could use the brains that got us into the Anthropocene to enact the scientific solutions already available to avert disaster. For three decades I have hoped. I voted, I protested, I lowered my environmental impact. I believed in reason and humanity. I hoped for the change that surely would come. That we would want our grandchildren to survive, even if we didn't care about the rest of life on earth.

Now, I don't hope. I despair. I try not to feel my grief and rage, because it feels unbearable.

I love this earth our home. I love the neon flick of indigo fish between rose and sapphire coral. I love the songs of birds and frogs as twilight deepens. I love the turning of the seasons, the glitter of frost, the riot of autumn leaves, the smell of spring wattle, and summer rain on hot dirt. I love the twisted limbs of riverside eucalypts, the moss and humus composting in forests, the sigh of wind between mountain boulders scabbed with lichen. I love my world, my people, my kids.

I love.

I grieve.

I love.

Looking for the River

Kay Carins

We're in the street,
where the old Astoria once stood,
and it's late afternoon and nearly dark
when he tells me he went looking for the river
where we caught fish and frogspawn—
taking them home in buckets,
forgetting them when they died.

And although the place is different now
(for nothing stays the same, or only in our minds)
he'd found a way in, through the dog rose, thorns and nettles,
the burdening, brambling overgrowth of the years.
And there's an excitement in his voice—
like a boy on the brink of a great adventure,
that *Boys' Own* journey to the source of all secrets, all life.

We talk of his writing,
the plan to write the novel, condensed now
to the more urgent target of one hundred pages,
each page to be imbued with sun and snow, fields and football,
all the icons of the past, mythologised
into a narrative both lyrical and pastoral, epic and mystical,
in the grand and tragic sweep of its conception.

Streetlights blink on,
push back against the growing blackness,
and the air contracts around us with the bone-deep cold of winter.
When we hug, I feel the thinness of his arms.
It's a long hug,
the kind that lets you know it's probably our last.

‘Dead Babies R Us’

Gemma Sidney

        shouts the sign in bold black letters.
My feet brought me here
yet now I am stuck, mesmerised
beneath the sign only I can read. Others pass us by unfazed.
Dead babies—right next to the dollar store
offering the shiniest most inexpensive items
always the promise of more, more: something breaks, buy another!
Step inside for simulacra galore.

Dead babies next to the shopping centre entrance
leading to the library, once my place of solace,
tainted now by those huge letters:
Dead Babies R Us.
That place where, months ago,
I lay supine as the technician found   a lack.
A black tunnel opened up
between my eyes and the screen.   ‘Too much blood… the sac—empty.’

That day I'd come from the library
borrowed books, borrowed thoughts, borrowed beliefs and pregnancy myths.
Confident, expert authors
casual claims when words can maim: 'Miscarriage one in four!'
That word doesn't seem to apply
to my lack   …complete and utter lack.
An absence of life is not death exactly
but something else—an in-between space   an emptiness.

I see the sign now for what it is: Perth Medical Imaging.
My feet release me, I step into the dollar store.
The bright lights catch on my teeth   …I am bared.
The shelves are ever full. I can get what I need here.
My hands grab at the wares, fill up my basket.
It feels good, this bringing together
of things once disparate. Yet when I turn to go
my basket is empty.

Bagging A Patient After Losing My Dad

Brown Woman

Two months after my dad's cardiac arrest, I found myself facing a patient's death. I had bagged numerous bodies during my time as a COVID-19 nurse in Naarm. I became skilled in comforting families and offering solace in their darkest hours. But now, the thought of touching death filled me with unfamiliar dread.

She died within an hour of my shift beginning. The room echoed with the wails of grieving loved ones as I moved in and out, offering what little support I could. The in-charge nurse urged me to take the body to the morgue, but I couldn't bring myself to rush her mob's farewell. One of the sisters stayed as we washed her body. Though masks weren't compulsory, I wore one to hide my tears. With each stroke, memories of my father's final moments flooded my mind. *Had he felt alone? Was he scared? Did he ask for us?*

As I murmured prayers under my breath, asking my Allah to look after her, I couldn't shake the image of my father being washed by the village men before his burial. *What did the men say to my dad when they washed his body?* I hoped they said comforting things. *Did Dad wonder where I was? Did they tell him your daughter is on a plane?*

You're okay, you're okay, you're okay. I murmured with every wipe across her still body.

Eventually, I had to bag the patient. The sister's fears mirrored my own, yet I pressed on, whispering words of comfort. Tears blurred my vision as I assured the patient that she can rest now. Walking her to the morgue, I envied her mob's chance to bid her farewell. It took me two and a half days to reach my homeland when my dad died, he was already buried when I got there. I never walked him to his death. Now, I imagined him in her place as I silently said my goodbyes. We walked past sliding doors, children holding the bed trolley.

Bye bye nana
Love you nana
Sleep well nana

Outside the morgue's doors, the weight of the final goodbye weighed heavy in the air. Men wept openly, their sorrow palpable. I joined them in their mourning. As I stood in my scrubs, I imagined this is how I would have said goodbye to my father, had he not died unexpectedly. I imagined the patient as my father. I said goodbye to her, but I also said goodbye to my dad. Through her, by her, and I got a sense that my dad felt it. I imagined our village men walking my dad to his grave, and this time I am walking with them, and I imagined my dad being less scared, having his daughter there with him. One of the elders said *palya, let us go.*

Returning to the ward, I saw a new admission being wheeled into the same room; the cycle of life and death continued unabated.

Spot

Tug Dumbly

A child's name for a dog, and it's the way my Mother says the childish name, Spot, the dog, 80 years gone, as she tells me how her brother, for a joke, put Spot on the big back bumper of a visiting Minister's departing car, but the dog never jumped, like he was meant to, he wasn't in on the joke, and got driven out the gate and down the road, the three children by now shouting and giving chase, but the deaf minister not hearing, not looking back, just the dog, cocking his head and wagging his tail, looking back at the children who are looking after a shrinking dust point down a country lane, after a disappearing Spot never to be seen again.

She's not sad as she tells me, but animated, younger, like she gets whenever she gives me a bit of real history, something beyond the quotidian trials of ageing. But her story hurts a bit to hear, like my Mother, with her hands of surfacing veins, mysteries of the body reaching ever closer, wanting to be told, like she is a little girl trapped in my chest, lightly rapping, politely tapping at every door and pane of that country town, beating like a little bird to get out, and it's vital that I, as a last keeper of her story, am stethoscope silent, to hear and feel every tiny knock. And there's more, so much more of her crucial history never to be told or done, but for now this crumb will do, and one day, maybe soon, Mum, there'll be a tempting bone, and Spot will find his way home.

The Wail

Ingrid Birgden

The raven squawked raucously as it circled the figure scrambling on all fours up the escarpment. An aircraft clattered overhead, gone as the boy waved the singlet he had rigged to the branch he had dragged across Wilpena Pound. He collapsed under a hopbush, dragging himself out of the searing heat. Turning onto his cheek he rasped, 'Help me, crow. I don't know where I am.'

At night outside the Pound, the mother comforted his three brothers before crawling into her tent, into the absence of her ten-year-old child. She curled into her pain. In the wake of every bitterly cold night, she crawled from the flashbulbs, the questions, the crowds. She crept into the dead centre of her dread and waited. Her breath ached. When the father of the lost boy entered their citadel and held her, she remained silent. The recriminations would begin later. Before long they would be living apart.

Each morning walkie talkies bleated on the lawns of Wilpena Chalet. The raven flew over the Adnyamathanha settlement of Nepabunna near the ranges to the northeast and was spotted wheeling overhead. An elder shifted the brim of his hat and called out, 'Clever black bird, tell us, where is the young fella?'

'They should have brought trackers in before the trail was trampled,' commented another, drawing a twig through the dirt.

'Poor boy's not in his country,' added a third, waving beyond the shade to the crags of scorched ochre.

In 1961, nearly three years later, human remains were discovered, exposed after a recent bushfire cleared the scrub. The leg bone was broken. There were remnants of a singlet tied to a stick. The boy's final resting place was on the side of St Mary's Peak, the highest in the Flinders Ranges and called Ngarri Mudlanha by the traditional owners. The name translates as waiting to take your mind.

In an Adelaide studio, his father, an art master, created a headstone as one last tribute. Against the contours of ancient landforms, he shaped a branch with its makeshift flag. Its signal had been a cry for help. He responded to his son's call from one beautiful and terrible world across to the next.

Alone after the ceremony in the Hawker Cemetery, retreating from slamming car doors, the eldest brother crunched back across the red shale to the memorial. He heard the wail of an Australian Raven as it descended into forlorn silence. It echoed his own grieving heart. The black bird landed on the headstone.

Watch over this nest for his bones, the teenager prayed, facing the raven. Later, as Premier of the state, friends claimed the arc of his public commitment was driven by the memory of his brother. He never once spoke of his death. With a heavy flap of its wings the bird flew away.

In the skies above Ikara-Flinders Ranges, the raven's lament still drifts down the generations for those who listen.

The day you left

Rachael Mead

In memory of Alison Flett

The sun didn't come up this morning, Adelaide gifting you one last taste of Scotland. Walking to the Botanic Gardens, everything is silvered and soft, revealing only what's right in front of me while the distance tucks its secrets away. I'm twenty minutes early. They are twenty minutes late. Any other day, irritation. But this morning, I wander in the fog, thinking of you, the stillness broken only by the carols of magpies. Lines are brewing, but I'm too ashamed to be caught turning your last minutes into a poem. But you? You'd be thinking poetry. And later, you'd bring it to our group, something with atoms or *umwelt* and a fox peering out through the black bramble of lines and we'd all be floored by what was going on in your head while we were debating where to get coffee. There'll be no later. A jogger runs past in full make-up, her body a perfect expression of youth and vitality and I think 'wait until middle age' then the gut punch of knowing that's all you got. Years ago, Heather gave us both a card with an old woman in a red polka dot bikini and wild sunglasses reading a book as she sat in a deck chair planted in the sea. *This will be us when we're old!* And now you are lying in your bed, surrounded by husband, kids and the boxed faces of your family on a screen. We stand in a tree-draped gazebo, holding each other, one of us a crying face cupped in an iphone as the moment ticks by. The candle-flame wobbles, then lives on. I can't stop thinking something should happen. The flame guttering to smoke. Foxes streaking around the cup rim in an amber blur. We wander away for coffee and the sun burns through as we pass our grief back and forth between us. Walking through the city, it's a new world. Everything is you but the tense has changed. The yellow of that knitted headband you loved. To loop my leather backpack over both shoulders will now be Alison-style. Every Parklands cyclist is you standing on the pedals as you pushed off towards home. I pass two Christians with their pamphlets and Laminex display of smiling white faces and I want to kick it to shards. I want to scream in their faces what sort of god? I want to gnaw on the bones of my life. Driving home in my hatchback, a ladybird flies in. It creeps through the dust of the dash. Trying to save it, I knock it into the footwell where it's lost among the sand, bakery bags and keep cups. But no—here it is—shiny spotted wings the exact orange and black of that mod dress I gave you when you first got that pixie cut. And you looked so freaking beautiful at that poetry reading at Heather's as we sipped afternoon light from our wineglasses. I remember it was getting dark and we were sitting together under the low heaven of party lights as a poet read from her iphone. She'd lost her place and was scrolling and scrolling and we grinned at each other as the pause stretched into an uncharted space beyond awkward. And I can't remember if the light hitting your cheekbones was from the moon or the strings of tiny stars, but I'll hold that moment forever—the dark thickening but you somehow still shining as the poet kept scrolling and scrolling and scrolling because she couldn't find the words.

After the Fire

Maggie Jankuloska

I drove past your house today. Call it habit or a magnetic pull, but I meandered through the dirt roads yet again to reach what was left of you.

I still expected to see your boots by the front door, sturdy and manky after a day's work. You didn't appear by the mailbox or front door, no hand zealously raised to welcome me in, to show me the goats and wine barrels, your pride and joy. Instead, traces of the fire were everywhere.

In the unnerving silence, I was hit by your absence, the magnitude of it. Nothing would be the same now.

Why were you so obstinate? You knew you couldn't fight it off, couldn't save the livestock and the buildings. Buildings were just buildings, brick and mortar, they could be replaced. The fire didn't care about how many decades you'd spent on the land; it didn't quake in fear at your tenure over the acres. It just took. It took you too. Did you rage until your last breath at an enemy as old as time?

What remained of your house stood crookedly, charred and adorned in graffiti, initials of young lovers in neon love hearts. New stories upon the old and dead ones. Someone had squatted in the surviving rooms and splayed up ugly curtains, I knew you would have hated them. Hated the mere thought of anyone being in your space, on your hallowed ground.

Birds chirp and swoop. The sun's heat scorches my neck. The grass is dead and the acrid smell of the fire's hunger lingers. Your footprints on the well-worn soil are gone, but I'm sure you are still somewhere near, in some new form. Imprinted on the soil and the trees. You're on the flowers as they begin to bud.

Epitaph

Michelle Brock

A young wombat is lying belly-up
stiff legs towards the sky

motionless

like a child's cuddle-toy
flung from of the window
of a passing car.

Stray breezes rouse
its soft brown fur.

Soon the stench of decay will wrap its flesh
and scavengers and detritivores will pick its bones.

What cravings lured it from earth's warm embrace
to cross the road beneath the crescent moon?
What foraging delights remain undisturbed on the other side?
Kangaroo grass? Tussock? Roots?

Was it stunned by the headlights of a passing car?
Spotted too late for the driver to slow down?
Collateral damage of a fast-food delivery?

Did someone stop to witness its demise
or did they drive on

oblivious

or perhaps pull over
momentarily
to inspect their car?

grief work / heaven in a mayonnaise jar

Taneshia Atkinson

the residue of your existence
(or the screeching of your absence)
bears such a weight to this day
that at first
it
          was
                    so
                              intense
I thought I was going to grow your bones if I cried hard enough
I listened to the wind for your voice
(I still do)
with such vigour that I thought my skull would collapse.
red wine curdling from my insides to meet and dance across the shower floor
each sip before, like I was drinking you in
          (the only time I thought you were palatable)
I smoked a pack of cigarettes in your name
charred throat
stained fingers
          a reflection of you

and now you sit
in a mayonnaise jar
wrapped in twine
          (tightly, as if it were my holding heart together)

it's foolish to think you're on my top shelf
because nomadic spirits never remain in one place.

your absence still screeches
but I've given up on growing your bones.

Renovation

Frances Horne

I choose Egg-shell™ so as
not to offend.

I prep slowly, stir love
songs into the paint

& start where things ended,
in the family room.

I roll heartache into each wall, over-
lapping each vertical stroke.

I am liberal, there are drips.
But I will not miss a spot.

With each coat
the rooms become lighter;

white's eerie love song
to space

redraws dimensions.
Our small rooms expand

as if all the songs are blues
standards, each room
a meditation
on longing.

Painting the ceiling is hardest,
as if I'm erasing the sky.

I leave the bed-
room as is.

After

Tim Loveday

we softened earth with shoe point
wove blisters on our fingertips with the loose
threads in our trousers, traded rollies for nips
from the silver flask—our faces refracted in
the lawlessness, we hovered in the dying
light, dying all around us.

After, there was four not five & the last
time I saw you was the last time forever:
your rollerblades slung over your shoulders
the fairy lights like an MDMA halo, you told me
about the fifty-foot blue-gum that you & your father
felled. The commercial acrobatics & the tension
of the winch. The whooping of the limbs.

After, I weighed the heaviness of headlights
& the whine of tyres & the way a wheel can *just*
jump, as I sat through court proceedings, the baritones
of court officials, the pleas, the impact statements, the evidence,
the verdict. All the while the girl who was no older than us or
your brother—boy who waited in the half light, boy whose shirt
was dark crimson when they found him—became
the victim of your death, not you.

After, I knew the exact spot where it happened, slowed for
the bend. Tried to avoid it. Who would ever walk there again?
So close to your parents' house. So close to the veranda where
we stayed up on sticky nights & played Tekken. The hot smoke
of a bong hovering in a chamber. How it all just disappears. We
talked of getting out, moving on. We talked of our futures. We
talked of other places. We talked about after. We
talked. Anywhere, but here.

An Always Unexpected Day

Barbara Ascoli

I take a breath. *Oh no. Oh no.*

I knew this was coming but the unpredictable end of another's breath is rarely planned.

My next surprise is my calmness.

Let's get on with the day. This walk. I'm fine.

The forest walk is thousands of kilometres from my home and my brother's home. I look at the wide girth of these trees and their strong roots that surface amongst the thick under-storey. Their cycles of growth remind me of our limited time on this earth. How we need to take that oxygen deep into our souls and bodies, so that we have the energy and capacity to extend our limbs to the sun and grow through all the darkness. This damp mulch gives the nourishment and moisture to build this forest. I also see the remnants of fire, that sister grief that burns into every part of us. Some seeds only re-generate with fire. Maybe we can too? With time? With love? With support?

I am searching for a tree with three branches. Three siblings that grew from the mulched kindness, love and hospitality of parental goodness. One dead, and one who is slowly leaving us with Alzheimer's. I miss being able to share our family stories. She would have cried with me today.

And laughed with me when a cousin notified our extended family of my husband's death instead of my brother's. I had to quickly rectify that error before my walk, as my concern was that some older cousins (who do not use mobile phones) may phone my home line for funeral details, with my husband answering.

'No worries,' he says, 'I'll just tell them, I came back because I didn't like where I went.'

I catch my breath. Watch my steps. I am not young anymore, but I will not admit to being old. I am OK, alone on this path. I finally find my tree and, in the shadows, surprise myself as I start to shake and sob loudly. Not lost on this track but lost for the rest of my living days. The finality of death hits me now, as I feel the hardness of the wood, smell the damp earth, and hear the forest sigh and groan with me. This forest knows life and death. It knows it all. I know so little.

On the day of my brother's funeral (that I cannot attend due to distance) my granddaughter takes me to her favourite beach. I kneel on the white sands, rather than on a church pew, when I give thanks for my brother's life. So many tidal forces connect our days. I will recall more of those days when my grief subsides. Now I just value each breath and what is around me. And live an amazing, ordinary, everyday life.

FILM TREATMENT FOR A PIXAR SHORT

J. Taylor Bell

i've lived in quite a few tin cans over the years, but only once was there ever a break in, and the only thing those crooks stole was a pair of shoes, which came as quite a relief because the day before i'd just stepped in dog poo, which was why they were by the door in the first place, nike airs, nothing special all things considered, sometimes you've got to be glad you've got the back room, and it's well that we don't know the last time we see something will be, otherwise we might disgorge a generous portion of our lives performing the ceremonies associated with saying goodbye, imagine all the wreaths, deflated pool rafts, catered wake sandwiches, hours on a phone erasing all of the chats & contacts across different platforms, sabermetrics is still asking why darvish altogether stopped throwing his slow curve & i remember dollar hotdog night when we watched the air go out of it like a what do you mean he's dead, and now it's tuesday afternoon at the cinema and toy story 4 has been out since we got the ashes back, i'm at the ticket window but something doesn't feel right, besides the fact that it's not christmas and a year can't feel like a day but a day can feel like a year, if you don't believe me when was the last time you watched the director's cut of eyes wide shut or baseball on fox sports, the last place we ever saw each other was LA of all places, gridlocked in the backseat of an uber and a broken fingernail in a bowling ball in koreatown, i can't believe you're giving me shit for not being able to finish a subway sandwich, when kershaw pitches dodgers tickets disappear like hours on a plane flying towards a tragedy, wondering who at that moment was wearing my stolen pair of shoes, and what ever became of my childhood, ask not from whom the bells stole, the matinee costs the same as a pack of junior mints, and if it's true that it only takes a few minutes to make a man, then it takes even less to break him, and sometimes when i look into things like the popcorn cube or empty screens i'm seeing a reflection that seems defined just by what it's seen departing, goodbye my hairline, adios my resolve, hello sweet imitation liquid butter dispenser, i never thought i'd be wishing to hear again about how hot it was today in texas, how the yard is starting to shape up, the non-activities of which early retirement consists, every day is the hottest day of the year, 365 days, one sun revolution since the last whatsapp message i sent, asking whether he'd received the margaritaville dvd we bought him off amazon, and his reply, which i've turned into my own personal epitaph, a thing i'll spend the rest of my life walking away from:

sorry
haven't seen it

Pain Travels With Me

Sally Jane Smith

In the Basilica Cistern of old Constantinople stands a green-tinged pillar. Its surface is carved with eerie teardrops, commemorating the slaves who died building this sunken palace of lifegiving water. The stone glistens with moisture, sorrow seeps from every pore.

Wherever I go, Türkiye weeps with me.

The street animals seem drawn to my sadness. There are fleeting moments of solace in the company of the dog curled on my doormat in Göreme, and the cat that shares my evening iftar meal, breaking our fast in a lonely park. On a quiet path beside Bursa's Grand Mosque, a kitten plays among my skirts as they flutter in the breeze. She arches her spine against my leg, pressing her head into the soft fabric. In the deserted lanes of Cumalıkızık, when the weight in my breast brings me to the ground, a warm tongue to the nape of my neck shocks me out of the hollow despair that threatens to consume me. The puppy dances around my body in mischievous delight as I crouch on the cobbles, and I hear the echo of Carly's raucous laugh.

Wherever I go, Türkiye presses her hand to my heart, holding my grief close.

The hills of Gallipoli are scored with narrow paths, trodden into the earth by ANZAC stretcher-bearers as they climbed from hospital ships to battle trenches and back again. I pick my way between thistles and thorns, following the trail left by the hooves of donkeys laden with damaged flesh.

Wherever I go, Türkiye walks alongside me, bearing my burden.

A mist of rain floats over Konya, Rumi's city, like a fine cloak hanging from the shoulders of the Sufi master. Surrounded by praying women, bending, rising and touching their foreheads to the floor, I sit back on my heels and let my head drop low, watch silent tears drip onto my folded hands. Outside, white gravestones rest in the long grass as a ray of silver fractures heavy clouds, and the poet's words break open deep inside me: 'The wound is the place where the light enters you.'

** Note: The quote in the last line is widely attributed to the thirteenth-century poet and scholar Jalāl al-Dīn Muhammad Rūmī, more often referred to as Rumi.*

Show me where it hurts

Cia Lawerence

I look at my ten-year-old son's face. It's drawn, and pale; the skin under his eyes dark. His father and I have been keeping the truth from him for over a week, maintaining the pretence that everything is business as usual at home. Mum's just been sleeping on the couch because dad snores. The arduous new kitchen job she's started working is just for fun.

Everything is fine.

Except that it isn't and because he's a sensitive child, bright and compassionate, he knows that something very serious has been happening around him; feels the grief that radiates from both of his parents as we eat meals, watch television, and tuck them into bed at night. Our shredded nerves have torn his in kind. I see it.

When he asks his voice is tremulous yet hopeful, desperately seeking the sweet relief of reliable sameness.

He has grown up in a home where the fighting can span hours. Although he and his brother have been allowed to watch more TV or play videogames, I doubt our efforts at distraction ever counted for much.

Emerging from behind closed doors with eyes swollen shut from tears, I could always feel that they understood we were collectively negotiating the wreckage of another conflict. They'd be meeker. Only children, yet trying so hard to reduce the tension—to be good boys.

'Mum, are you and dad getting a divorce?'

Even on the worst days I have managed to plumb the same answer from beneath the weight of rolling nausea and blackest self-loathing. Those magical words. No, of course not.

'Let's talk about it when we get home,' I croak instead.

'Mum, *are* you?'

There's mounting desperation in his voice, and my stomach churns as I gauge our surroundings.

My youngest son is galloping across the oval with his soccer mates in preparation for their weekend match. The OSCH kids are scaling the distant play equipment, screaming and laughing in the crisp winter air.

None of them know that my eldest boy's world is about to collapse because I just can't lie to him anymore.

I answer, honestly at last, and can only guess at the devastation I've wrought. His pain is his own, yet the impact is instantly visible. My boy's face crumples. He falls into my arms, sobbing, begging:

'No, no, no!'

I hold him tightly; smooth his hair. My chest is aching and my own eyes are wet, but I bite back sobs.

I recognise that this moment will be with him forever, even though I'm hopeful that he will heal around it in the future. Regardless of how wonderful life may be beyond today, this memory will remain one of profound loss.

As his mother I feel compelled to witness what my choice has cost him and accept the weight of his grief as the rawest part of my own. I couldn't hate myself more than I do now.

But then, I still have to tell his brother.

The Moon on my Verses

Juan Garrido-Salgado

Beautiful! With traces of the purest and most innocent Lorca's influence.

Victor Hugo Romo

The moon bites my verses
on this night of absence
I bark my vowels
I chase its consonants.
My dreams are frightened of abyss
I lie exhausted on the dark shore
where the silence of the world murmurs
on that sad corner
a fleeting light drags the pain
among the rubble in Gaza

Writing from the intimacy of interstitial tissues

Anne M Carson

...it has been profoundly healing and transformative to be able to reach
into and release stories that have been buried in my body, so I may dance
and re-story them by rewriting myself and reimagining society anew.
Sandeep Kaur Glover

She recounts her first visit to her motherland   the Punjab   tells us
the snake-bite kit   in her luggage   represents   fear

of her homeland learnt at school   poverty   backwardness
danger   She travels with her mother to the family village

On her first night   human murmurs   animal moans   wake her
She joins her family downstairs   where a heifer bellows

in distress   The animal strains   breath ragged   limbs shuddering
Her calf is bodying   through the birth canal   forcing tissues apart

cervix dilating   The whites of the gravid mother’s eyes show
Gathered around the family chant   as they have always chanted bovine birth

an embodied practice   for their revered family member   When two
hooves push through   the exhausted mother   surrenders to gravity

folding down to be   held by the maternal earth   The mothers
know what she is going through   what it costs   in endurance

to grow life inside   in pain   to push it out by the muscle
of one’s own   female will   I wonder how the chant

lands for the cow   I imagine her   deep inside her own birth dreaming
held in a field of support   dirt under her flank   familiar human touch

and smell they who praise her   paint her beloved horns and forehead
now wrap her   in the softly persuasive vowels of kinship

Oh mother-to-be   we love you   beautiful   strong
soon the pain will cease   soon you will be eating grass
soon your calf   will nuzzle you   drink your milk

Never a mother myself   never knowing such cultural wisdom
I long to be there   with the humans   chanting to the cow mother

I can't find this practice   on the UNESCO register   but I want it recognised
protected   part of   *The Intangible   Cultural Heritage   of Humanity*

'Writing from the intimacy of interstitial tissues' is a quote from Sandeep Kaur Glover, 'Fleshing Out the Embodied Potentialities of Positionality' in *Qualitative Inquiry* 2024, Vol. 30(2) 154-–162. Retrieved DOI: 10.1177/10778004231176100 journals.sagepub.com/home/qix. This story was recounted by Sandeep Kaur Glover and this poem is written with her kind permission.

what the trees know

Jaya Penelope

after *Learning from Trees* by Grace Butcher

...and I will apprentice myself
to whatever it is the trees know
when they are undone.

I will stand stripped back
and thirsty, my hands raised
to the sky, my skin tattooed

with eyes, my rootlets
ghosting lost wetlands.
I will drink from buried

lakes, taste the chorus
of tannins and chlorophyl
on my tongues.

And when the honeyeater's nest
is blown from the branches
and the hatchlings lie helpless

and maimed on the path
well, they say even the Buddha
met death beneath the bodhi-tree's

branching canopy
and did not turn away.

To Carry

Emily Bridget Taylor

The week I find out I am pregnant, I see coyotes everywhere. On tee shirts. As discarded plastic toys on the pavement. A flesh and bone coyote runs along my vision on a clear night in New England. These are good omens, Mum says. These mean protection. Family. A pack. Soon you, baby, will join my pack.

The first time I see you, you are a pale circle of light against a fuzz of grey. My American doctor does not confirm that this is you. He tells me another specialist will call, to let me know. But I know. My circle of light. My child. Showing up in the glow of a coyote yellow moon.

In the weeks following, two people who are planners by nature find themselves struck still by the heralding of your arrival. We stumble over words. Compose texts. Take tests. Vulnerable silences—are you happy? *Yes.* Soon, we make plans. Plans and plans and plans. Lists of names, how to tell and who. A softness forms between us in the shape of you.

Some days the excitement slips to worry. I think of what I will lose. Time. Agency. The ability to work without feeling sick. This wasn't planned—and every day, I lose capacity. But then, I also grow in capacity. It's a dance. And despite the occasional moments of anxiety, I feel released. Released, at last, from just caring about me. Released from the disappointments of the past. Your miracle relegates *everything* to the land of Before.

Travelling home to Australia, we are unable to wait. We call family members from the airport. No way, they scream, exploding in excitement. I get tee shirts made with embroidered family names. These are wrapped on my friend's dining table, nervously carried to a pub, and met with tears of surprise once removed from the multicolour paper.

But then, within a few days of landing, there is blood.

GP visits, ultrasounds and tests are carried out—all return inconclusive. When I go home, the new moon washes the sky black. My abdomen cramps. I know it isn't good.

Soon, the blood comes with a vengeance.

Things pass through my body that I have never seen before. Things like the curd of milk and pomegranate seeds. I am self-revolted. I want to keep it in. *Stay in*, I whisper. But it can't and it won't. It washes out helpless—carried by the tide, lost to the sea.

Epilogue—

What is it to carry?
To hold, to be entrusted, to take care of.
I carry you
and you carry me—
it has only been six weeks
but your circle of light
on sonographic abyss
tells me you can feel
all
of
this.

We carry
the tears, the change
We carry
the late-night calls and questions
We carry
the graft
of two ancestral vines
and we carry your father's smile
in the hospital line.

Together, we carried—
it was not just *me* who carried *you*.

Drive

Seeth Dodd

Your fingers tremble on the steering wheel. Your knuckles are pale; your eyes are fixed ahead. This is no ordinary journey. You are driving behind your father's hearse. You concentrate on keeping the right amount of distance between you and him. But what is the right amount of distance? You were far apart for so long.

The clouds are a pallid grey, and the rain begins to fall. For one, wretched moment, you consider stepping on the accelerator. If you crash into the hearse, perhaps you could quantum leap the two of you into a different world. But you don't of course. You are a grown-up and must do as grown-ups do. Your father is watching.

Someone did offer to drive. You declined. After all, this is your final chance to prove your worth. This is how you show your dead father you are not inconvenienced by emotion. You are made of steel and mettle, and not of raindrops that dissolve at the slightest hint of pressure.

The rain collides with the windscreen, and you let it blur your vision for as long as you can bear it. You cannot bear it for long. Your father is in front of you. There is no room for error. There is no allowance for tears. Wipers flick back and forth. Their rhythm is a pacemaker for your anxious heart.

You keep both hands on the wheel. You are in control of nothing else. You must steer yourself now. You must gather the pieces of you and haul yourself into a new realm.

The crematorium appears through the grey. You do not want to arrive, but you cannot keep driving. Your father has stopped. The distance between you is closing.

Grief

Tom Dauven

She sits on the floor trembling

Shaking, as if roughly handled by God

She who has become grief.

She who lost her mother a month ago

And now her only son

Thirty-six and a heart attack.

No words, no words

We have come with the Quaker's gift of silence.

While she sits on the floor

Rocking back and forth

Moaning as if giving birth.

This woman who sits there making hard noises.

This woman giving death to her son.

One year, Six months, Two days

Adele Hally

The last period is science. I scrape my sister's name into the desk with the sharp point of my compass, scoring the letters into deep grooves. It is easy to imagine her laughing when she sees it—when she comes home. In the deserted quadrangle, an empty chip packet blows slowly and gracefully across the concrete, and I can't look away. The room is hot, and smells of stale sweat and rotting apples. The fans hum and click but don't disturb the syrupy air. The afternoon is heavy, and we are thick and torpid.

****

My mother is holding my hands. I want to go, and she keeps talking. I try to pull away, but she is surprisingly strong.

'Stay. Stay and talk with me for a bit,' she says. I think she has been drinking.

'You have beautiful hands. Long and delicate fingers,' she says stroking my palm.

'Your sister had lovely hands too.'

'Has,' I say, yanking my hand out of her grasp.

'What?'

'*Has*. She *has* beautiful hands!'

'Oh sweetheart, please stay and talk with me.'

She sighs as I walk away.

****

3 am and I have forgotten how to sleep.

I walk around the house in the dark, trailing my fingers along the walls to keep my bearings. Everything is unfamiliar in the night. This place that I have lived in for my whole life feels fragile, an elastic space where perspectives and proportions are all wrong. Dogs begin to bark along the street—a warning. Seconds later, a gust of wind slams into the side of the house like a punch. A southerly buster roars in from the ocean dropping the temperature in an instant. Leaves and sticks clatter down on the metal roof in a wave of sound. The whole house shudders, the windows rattle their frames, everything creaks and is suddenly alive.

In the bathroom, I pick through the chaotic mess of objects in the vanity drawer. Strands of my sister's long blonde hair twist around a purple scrunchy and I use it to tie a ponytail—her hair mingling with my own. Rain hammers the bathroom window, and the gale sounds like a woman wailing. It sounds like heartbreak.

I pick up a bottle of lip gloss. Hers. Her favourite. It is strawberry-flavoured, the smell is intense and sweetly artificial. I roll it onto my lips, breathing in the scent, coating my mouth in a thick shiny slick. As I inhale deeply, over and over, I can see her. I see her wide laughing mouth, her lips shimmering, her bright light, her wildness. Her absence.

She loved this lip gloss.

A LIFE DISMANTLED.

Mary Salter

All around us was the accumulation of a lifetime. The glass cabinets housed knick-knacks, treasures even—crystal glassware which we used to ping with our fingernails to hear that distinct, shiny ring; the framed certificate of a blessing from Pope Pius X; the Dutch pottery lady in a billowing skirt which hid the tinkling chime of a bell. Of what use now?

Now that Dad has finally followed Mum.

When Mum died, we moved nothing. Everything remained proudly on display. After all, it was still Dad's home. The mementoes of trips taken together became part of the décor and so the life they'd shared continued on in this room.

Now these keepsakes, so proudly assembled, invested with memories, have become simply, things. It was time for them to go too. We began the sad task of choosing or farewelling the once cherished reminders of journeys taken long ago.

'Does anyone want this cut glass trifle bowl from Poland?'

'I'd like that cup and saucer from their trip to London.'

'Who wants this crucifix?' It seemed somehow irreverent to put it in the throw-away box, even though we'd all dispensed with our childhood religion.

'Put it in that box for the second-hand shop.'

'Remember when they came back from Asia with all those chopsticks? They're still here in their boxes!'

We laughed as we remembered Mum who'd been brave enough to have her photo taken with a giant python round her neck, all of us declaring that we wouldn't have done it.

One by one, object by familiar object, we narrowed down their lives, until there was almost nothing left. The paintings had come down, the barometer and the hallway mirror. The walls were bare, with odd-shaped patches of things which once had filled up space.

The house began to echo.

Arriving there the following morning, on opening the front door, there was silence. No radio blared out the latest news. No leftover aroma of bacon from breakfast wafted from the kitchen. No happy hellos called out. All evidence of them had disappeared. The emptiness was palpable.

I'd been to the funeral house to identify Dad. Lying there in his coffin, I was shocked by how small he looked; how fragile, almost child sized. It seemed that his spirit had not only invigorated him, but had also enlarged him, given him heft as though the body I beheld could not contain him any longer. He'd broken out of his shell; left it empty.

And this was what came back to me as I opened the door. I was inside an overwhelming emptiness. It felt lonely. Tears filled my eyes. I cried in sadness for all that had gone. But I also cried with relief; that they'd both found freedom. No longer housed, no longer constrained. Untrammelled, they'd flown. Finally free of a world filled with things.

The Grim Sister

Alexandria Scott

In another universe, my brother is not buried with his braces on.

Instead, he turns seventeen and our family gathers at the local bowling club to celebrate. Joyful and ravenous for greasy, hot chips and good conversation, we push tables together and claim seats, leaving him at the head. Embarrassed, he follows me to the bar, eager to escape the attention and the heat of his cheeks. I buy him a Coke and he leans heavily against my shoulder as we wait for our drinks to arrive. He is a head taller than me and growing, next year I'll be shouting him a beer.

Once dinner is consumed and all tales have been told, someone turns off the lights. A store-brought mud cake is brought out to the tune of 'Happy Birthday' sung in horrible harmonies. The candles illuminate his face, a halo of light in a darkened room, our grandmother tells him to smile for the camera before making a wish. He smirks, his top lip slipps awkwardly over the delicate wires glued to his teeth. He has time.

In another universe I never have to ring the orthodontists' office. I never cancel my brother's appointment. I do not hide in my mother's walk-in closet to muffle the sounds of sobbing from another room. And when the receptionist asks if I'd like to reschedule for a later date, I would not have to explain.

Reality is grief's grim sister, and I cannot escape her. Sat at a table at our local bowling club, my family pushes food around their plates. We're rehashing conversations that we've had thousands of times before, when someone says: 'he wouldn't have liked adulthood anyways.'

Bitter and traumatised, I feel strongly that he still deserved the chance to know.

The Heart of the Matter

Kel Titchmarsh

After

My name is Kel. I survived heart attacks last August.

I don't know how much of Before Kel has been erased by this: what facets of my life I'll be able to go back to, what activities have become *used to*s.

I already felt afraid in environments because of my Autism.

Now I also feel afraid in my own body.

But time is passing. And time has a way of firmly rubbing my back and reassuring me. Every day is a day further away from the heart attacks, every day lengthens my streak of being safe and alive.

I'm learning to trust time.

I'm learning to make eye contact with my heart.

I'm learning to make eye contact with my life.

During

Shock. My words stuck on spin cycle, apologising for unknown crimes.

Was this actually how I was going to die? Was I dying?

Blood thinners and patchwork memories, anaesthetic and no routine.

My life didn't flash before my eyes. What I *did* see were the people I loved, my fur babies, my godsons. I know the pain of being left behind.

I still struggle to accept that this wasn't on purpose, a series of choices I made in an act of unloveableness. But the choices weren't up to me, they were up to the emergency room, then coronary care.

Hospitals are the exact opposite of my safe environments. Chaotic, noisy, brightly lit.

My brain engaged in a wrestling match against itself, arguments being presented in fast staccato pace:

Escape!

I have to stay.

I can't do this!

I have to do this to find a way through this.

Smells! Noise! Unfamiliarity!
Heart.

Before

Protecting my postoperative stomach in the car, a bigger problem reared its head: I was crushing from the inside out, chest collapsing in on itself, pain pain, pain.

My body was betraying me. My heart, breaking.

I kept saying *It feels like ten out of ten,* but I do tend to get stuck on loops when I'm distressed.

The plan: assume it was post-operative pain, medicate, curl up with my fur babies three.

The pain became easier to tolerate, knowing it was post-operative pain.

Until Monday.

That Monday.

It felt like my teeth were falling out, like my neck was actively choking me, like my breathing was a mechanism under construction, fragile in function due to the tightness of the chest that contained it.

That driftwood has so many chambers. The whole is made up of so many holes.

Something was wrong with one of my chambers.

I'd been having heart attacks.

I was surprised until I wasn't. I kept asking *how could this have happened?*

Family history. Eating disorder. A really big stomach surgery. Fur baby venturing over the Rainbow Bridge.

How could it not?

With the flick of a switch, my body was drained of strength and energy.

In the flick of the same switch, I became a heart attack survivor.

Airstrike Ghazal

Ronald Atilano

> 'Going to the hospital meant risking our lives.'— a mother in Gaza, *The Guardian*, 29 December 2023

A rocket is falling, about to strike a hospital.
A rocket that knows the coordinates of the hospital,

Sees the names on its registry, the aged and wounded,
The young and near-death, they who seek salvation in the hospital.

The rocket peers into each room, into each bed.
A lightning of missiles illuminates the hospital.

Here is a child with a bloodied head,
Awake by the window. A fountain of night flares bathes the hospital.

A doctor amputates an old man's leg.
The rocket hears a flurry of feet up and down the hospital.

In the nursery, the hum of a mother's breath,
The thunder of rockets rocking babies to sleep in the hospital.

In the ICU, the simplicity of flatlines, the rise and ebb
Of heartbeats. The rocket traces its parabola towards the hospital.

Who sleepwalks in the hallway with the grieving and the dead
As the rocket nears? All clocks are chiming in the hospital.

And here I will leave the poem: a rocket hanging by a thread,
Eternally falling, just a shooting star passing, like a child's wish, over a hospital.

The Way of Grief

Maria Solano

This story begins and ends with me.

As I reach the halfway point of my life's journey, I also reach the point where I have lived half my life with chronic illness, and grief is its unwanted companion.

The foundations were laid *in utero* when mother felt unloved, and father was never home; usually with another woman. I was born into grief, loss, abandonment, betrayal, and emotional unsafety, exacerbated by father attempting suicide when I was six months old. My pure, innocent soul became burdened by a toxic emotional overload.

Childhood was the grief of rejection by father, silenced by mother: peace must be kept and rules obeyed.

School was an overwhelming and painful kaleidoscope of being bullied, making friends, but anxiety not allowing for those intimate female friendships I so desperately needed. Feeling too unworthy, unfocused, in survival mode. I craved to be seen, heard, accepted, loved.

By twenty-three, my body was showing subtle signs of suffering. A specialist appointment left me in tears as I was told it would be wise to turn off my ovaries for a prolonged period. Did I want children, was I worthy of children, could I be a good mum?

I developed viruses, infections, a myriad of exploratory surgeries. My body was crying its grief out in an explosion of painful, broken ways. I felt everything, but at the same time felt nothing. I could not feel into my body to heal being so shut down, so I stayed in my head. My body eventually decided for me.

One day I awoke and felt literally paralyzed. My head was weighted down, and I struggled to get the rest of my body off the bed and my feet on the floor. I turned up to work gasping for air and my brain felt like it was on fire, physically and cognitively. A doctor diagnosed me with chronic fatigue syndrome. My body had had enough. I had failed it.

I spent the next twenty-five years collecting more health disorders along the way, losing my ability to drive, work, maintain friendships, relationships, take care of myself. A never-ending waterfall of grief cascaded down upon me accepting this new way of life, of being, becoming a bit player in my own life story. I had to wipe the board clean of dreams, experiences, companionship, and work with what I had left.

The grief is always there in the background poking its sorrowful head in to say hello. In spite of its constant entanglement in my being, I have produced saleable art while lying in bed, published stories, and continued to learn, inspire, be inspired. I have never given up hope of improving my life, and I will not allow grief to consume me to the point that it drowns me under its defeat. I am not helpless. I am not nothing. Grief walks beside me. It has shaped me, shifted me, and it has taught me.

Why We Do Welfare Checks

Robert Prudence

It was some twenty years ago now, but this is still burned into my brain. A standard day, a standard vacant possession. John, an elderly man had fallen, went to hospital for several months and was declared fit to leave. But not fit to return home. So John was shuffled into twenty-four-hour supervised aged care. Slow wheels meant it was months before the paperwork was finalised and we could start the process of letting the unit out to someone else. My job was to gain entry, document, organise repairs and then manage the transition. A very typical process.

Standing outside the apartment, a putrid smell was seeping out from under the door. One last deep breath of fresh air then I fitted my filtration mask. Experience matters. My breathing harsh and noisy, I turned the purloined key. The force of the stench staggered me, even through the mask. Pungent. Powerful. My eyes watered. I stepped inside, camera flashing. No mail on the floor, not even a catalogue.

Kitchen first. No plates. No cups. No cutlery. A tiny card table with a red marbleised top and one green vinyl chair that had been liberated from an RSL club decades before. On the table was a single random novelty glass from some event fifty odd years previous. Hundreds of pill bottles though. All sorts, on every flat surface, inside cupboards, on benches, on the top of the fridge. I sealed the fridge, never to be opened again, just recycled. The bedroom was the same. A broken single bed, a couple of well-worn flannelette shirts and countless cigarette burns on the wall near the head of the bed, a mound of butts underneath.

The bathroom next, a horror show. The smell was immeasurably stronger, I had to run outside the unit, breathe, run in, photograph and run back out for the next breath. The floor was thick with congealed human slime. Very squelchy, every shade of brown with a little yellow, green and red pooling on surfaces. The toilet. The bath had several inches of a brown, wobbling jelly in the bottom. I dared not touch it.

But the disturbing room was the lounge. A busted chair with springs poking through it. An ironing board surrounded by iron burns. An ancient cabinet TV set. Mounds of cigarette butts. No photographs, but the walls were … wallpapered in thousands and thousands of birthday cards. Some old, some very new. All pasted to the wall, no space left. And on them, written in the same faint spidery handwriting—'To my darling husband John, Happy Birthday, Your wife Eloise'.

Back to the office to complete the paperwork. A decision needed to be made about his meagre effects. So at the round table with the nursing home and his caseworker, I asked about getting hold of Eloise to see if she might want anything. The answer—'Oh no, Eloise died decades ago, back when John retired'.

Dancing Inside a Prayer

Richard James Allen

The universe is shouting at me again tonight.
A few drunken retorts around midnight should suffice.

No use crying over spilt imagination.

My eyes are growing older than any other part of me.
My life is an installation in the real world,
press-ganged into the moment,
but my mind is elsewhere.

Line by line,
I have been building my defence
against the idea of light, the premise of light, *the whim of light...*

These mountains of reason,
decorating the streets
like sierras of garbage
during a sanitation workers' strike.

Sunsets are the grace notes on my days
along my boulevard of broken sleep.

I don't walk the dog, I walk the emptiness.

You can start death without me. I'll be along presently.
I'd like to avoid the rush.

Valediction.
Until our blue skies meet again.

The Lost Boy

Suzi Mezei

For Peter

The outcrops on Mars look like stacked slate and in the photo,
even the air seems tinged with red.   *You wave,*   ebullient

in boardshorts, your top-half bare,   the light from a
photographer's flash illuminates your child-features, a third of
your right foot buried in what I assume is sand, the kind
and colour just like the arkose grain we skimmed in Uluru. On
a quest   you scurry like a brown bug over mounds, scale crags
that look more ancient than the earth, but you never find the sea.
Not even a precious inch of skin gets wet. You look solitary
in most of the shots, though you write that the other boys

are simply out of frame hiding 'round the other side of cold
boulders: it's all just a game, you can hear them laughing,
their echo fills the crimson gaps where you loiter on the
long walk back home. It's getting late. Some nights, I dream
you back into the places where you should be, touch the rushing
heat that lurks beneath your thriving flesh, inhale the non-stop
momentum of a human bud unfurling; then in a flash it's gone
and your absence is as heavy as a Martian cairn   in the

epicentre of my chest. I decide to call you,   then remember
that,   ever reckless,   you left your phone behind.

Lost Identity, Lost Friend

Lisa Barron

Olivia changed from a peaceful hippy to an aggressive New Wave person when she moved to Redfern. I did not understand.

One night she played The Rolling Stones, 'Paint It Black,' full volume, all night and into the morning. Sunrise revealed everything was painted black—our front steps, the flowers in our front garden, the dining room table and absolutely anything that was small in our home. It also brought the smell smoke. It was coming from the Olivia's locked room. Sobs could be heard too. Our housemate convinced her to open the door. I stood nervously behind him. The smoke was billowing out of Olivia's slashed pillow. She was sitting on the bed watching it, sobbing with a carving knife in her hand. Olivia screamed at me, so I left to let someone else get to the bottom of the blackness.

Our house was condemned. Unknown to me, so was our friendship. Olivia and I went our separate ways.

I remained friends with her until her unpredictability became personal. Sometimes she stayed with us. One morning, I was greeted by flying lemons that were all targeted at me. Confusion and a great desire to protect myself initially made it difficult to comprehend what was happening. Olivia's voice brought clarity yelling, 'Sour lemons for a sour teacher!' Her voice stopped when I pinned her to the wall.

Other days she came to visit with a half empty bottle of Serepax, telling me that she had taken the other half. She said that she wanted to die and asked me to spend the day with her to stop her. What a challenge. We roamed around Redfern streets and railway tracks. A lot of non-judgemental conversation prevented her success and my trauma.

Our friendship became too much for Olivia. I triggered something deep in her. She could never explain it. I missed the gentle Olivia.

The next time I saw her she was wearing a singlet top with an aboriginal flag across the front of it. She told me, 'It turns out I am not part Spanish. I am Aboriginal. When I moved here everyone kept calling me sis and asked who my mob was. I told them that I was not Aboriginal but no one believed me. Eventually a woman told me to go to 'Link up' an organisation that connected aboriginal people to their ancestry. I'm aboriginal.'

I was stunned. I just listened as she told me that her father had told Olivia's Aboriginal mother not to admit that she was Aboriginal. Never. Her mother chose to be Spanish.

That was the last time I saw Olivia.

Everything made cruel sense then.

She painted everything black back then because she felt that the gaze of those people was painting her black, denying her Spanish identity.

Now I know that this is what happens when Aboriginality is denied.

Not My Boyfriend

Alexandra Grantham

On Brown Street, we walked into the lounge room on the second floor of his century-old terrace. There were five or ten people or maybe just one other person there, but someone handed me a drink and said, 'You don't have to do this if you don't want to.' In hindsight, it was a warning, but, at the time, it was a challenge. In defiance, I drank a lot, and I laughed too loud. I sipped the boxed wine just like I would with my mother's friends.

The music started buzzing in my head, in my ears, behind my eyelids. I had to sit and touch down on something real as my head disconnected from my body, distracted, dizzy, dark. He helped me lie down in his room; lights snapped, eyes blinked, blurred view, naked-numb, thrust upon, held down hostage. The paralysis stopped any sound as I fell back into unconsciousness.

At dawn, the sun sliced my face through the curtain. I memorised every detail of his room as I tried to find my bearings with a faint internal compass. I was cold, and he was naked beside me. I put my dress back on. It felt like barbed wire. Nausea spiked in my throat. I didn't want him as my boyfriend. He wasn't friendly at all. I repossessed my bra and underwear. I gripped them in a fist like they had betrayed me. I opened his bedroom door just as a siren pierced the silence.

'Oi, turn that thing off,' he yelled. I froze. 'I said, turn that off. Fuck!' He was angry I'd ruined his sleep. I didn't fumble; it was the same alarm clock I had as a kid. I dared to look at him to see what monster he was in the light of the day. He put a pillow over his head, blocking me out, and remained unknown.

Outside on the street, the world was barely functional. Street cleaners were muffled and indistinct in my ear. My feet barely touched the ground. I clenched my teeth as a stabbing, cold breeze couldn't console me. In my desert hometown, life was harsh, but you could trust people. I found myself in this surreal city, surrounded by millions, danger everywhere.

In my windowless bedroom, Kerry snored peacefully on our stained futon, unconcerned that I never made it home. I woke her to tell her what happened. She was the only person I ever told.

'You can't party with random men on buses, babe,' she paused and steadied herself. 'I would've told him to fuck off.'

'I couldn't,' I whispered.

'You're such a slut,' she joked and knocked my shoulder like we'd be laughing about it for years.

'I am not,' I looked away, shut down.

'Just another Friday night in the big city, hey?' she was still laughing as she left the room. So, I smiled too, but I never laughed.

My Mother's House

Janice Baker

In the kitchen, a pile of bedding—cushions, a pillow and rug for sleeping on the floor in front of the gas heater. Two couches host the most recent overflow from the other bulging rooms: handbags stuffed full of receipts; paper napkins; plastic cutlery; salt and pepper sachets; and pillars of paper that tremble and threaten to fall should you be foolhardy enough to try to sit down.

Clamorous towers shiver on every surface and on the floor: junk mail; religious pamphlets; rose magazines; historical society newsletters; bills; some red-emblazoned 'Final Demand' travel brochures; bank statements; receipts; local newspapers—in no discernible order or importance.

Kitchen cupboards store forgotten pots, crockery, cutlery, a little food. Next to the laundry sliding door, a small elderly fridge drones. Every so often it gives a thump, rests a while, lurches into droning again. On top are a microwave and kettle (the electric stove was buried under trays and shopping bags long ago).

Against the far wall is a small electric organ bought in the 1960s, that might wheeze if you tried to play it, on which rests a radio and small TV, one or the other always left on, loudly proclaiming either evangelical fervour or the news. On the walls are the plastic flower arrangements cemented into cheap wall vases made by my great aunt, while large photographs of Victorian relatives, dark, formal, unwelcoming, loom over the small aluminium café table and chairs, a chance for seating if only you could clear the clutter. Everything is covered with a gritty patina of dust, glued to each surface by years of condensation and boiled kettles.

On the sink lives a dish drainer with cups and glasses, two or three plates, microwave containers and cutlery. A few used teabags sit on a saucer, awaiting their second coming. In the slice of light through the grimy window, geranium cuttings sprout in a jar on the window ledge, swollen with roots.

This is my mother's house. As a child she had nothing but poverty, abuse and neglect; and as she grew she wanted everything, without discrimination, letting nothing go. Her eyes now have lost their focus, animated only with an anguish that I, cruel daughter that I am, might move something or take something away from her.

She sits in the corner in her soiled clothes, munching on takeaway chips, clearly annoyed and occupied with her own thoughts. There is no warmth, no welcome, no space and no place for me—she pushed me away years ago.

The Colours of Poppy

Bree Marsh

She collected voices, pinning them in her mind like a scrapbook. Each one had a colour. The high-pitched painful voices were ice blue and hard to look at. Poppy's voice was the deepest of browns, warm and delicious, and it was pinned to a place in her mind with the things that made her feel safe.

Poppy was gone now, they told her.

There are a lot of voices in the house today. Sickly green ones and the grating reds, mixed with purple-grey splotches of people sobbing. Too many colours. In the backyard there is only the breeze, and it's there that she chooses to spend the afternoon.

The garden is where Poppy first showed her the tiny smooth rocks. How to count them and put them in order from smallest to biggest. How to use them to make shapes, and sort by colour. Poppy didn't try to correct her when she grouped them by smell. One time they rolled the rocks off the table into a metal bucket, a funny sound that made them laugh all afternoon. Plink, plink, plink, plonk. Remembering Poppy's laugh made his voice colour an even more wonderful shade of brown.

They were always there, the rocks and Poppy. Now there were just rocks.

Sometimes she wondered about the colour of her own voice. She didn't use it much because of the way it made her ears feel. This was a big problem for most people—the less she spoke, the more they did. People don't like silence. But not Poppy, he never asked pointless questions like 'What's your favourite food?' That's not the way foods are pinned in her mind, foods are sorted by whether they're salty or if they're too loud to crunch. Likewise, she could never understand what was expected when someone asked how she was feeling or whether she was okay. A lot of people had asked her this today, with the pastel voices that told her something was wrong. She tried now to think hard about it. All she felt was a dull ache somewhere behind her stomach like when she forgets to eat.

Over time the voice colours fade a little, some even change to a different hue. Like the woman who sat behind her on the number 17 bus, with the tangerine voice that she had never seen before or since. When she remembered it now, the voice looked more of a dull orange. She wondered if Poppy's voice would stop being warm and delicious. She decided she would have to look at it every day to keep it fresh.

Plink, plink, plink, plonk.

If the people in the house should happen to glance down at the garden, they would see her sitting with her stockinged feet in the dirt, smelling the rocks and laughing to herself in the afternoon sun. Keeping the colours of Poppy.

Bad News Breaking

Richenda Rudman

I've left it late. Friday. Supermarket.
I tell myself: just in and out.
But my trolley fills—all that illuminance, all those colours rendered.
I bypass my slim list, yet hold fast for tissues: aisle 12.

A silver-plated couple hover near where I need to reach,
and the woman's hand grapples in her pocket for a ringing phone.
Her grip has not the easy yogic poise of her children,
she speaks loudly, listens hard,

then crumples, weighted sadness in each fold
as she hands the phone, like a smouldering ember,
to her husband, to whom she can only say the crumbs of words.
(Draw them as small dashes, little arcs and dots.)

I leave the scene: walking through someone's bad news is walking through their blood.
The aisle has lost its patency: other shoppers bump each other, do u-turns,
they look and don't look, living awkwardness in unlikely territory.
(Draw them with grey thought clouds, as zigzags and serrations.)

And someone with epaulettes is watching this upstairs live,
switching screens, from the back to the front, and to the sides of bad news breaking;
it is as rare as watching a moon landing—planets apart from steal-to-order steaks
in the meat section—that repeats itself—same trains leave the same station.

I pretend-shop elsewhere and return to aisle 12, where the call has ended,
but the couple remain on bypass; he stands at the midpoint of the aisle
and she takes creaking small steps away from him and back to him,
as if tethered, as if labouring a birth, trying to shift pain.
(Draw them as a dot and a small flat line, back and forth.)

I have no rope to throw them:
there are only the fragile, unreachable tissues—
nugatory, like spitting into an inferno.

Sunday

Stef Kokkinakis

Where did that voice come from,
the one that crackled from my lips
as you lay unconscious—

It's me, I'm here.
It's okay if you go, you can go, it's safe to go.

And when did the chorus enter,
echoing your mother's knowledge, firmer,
directing you—

Our baby,
you
must
go.

Labouring you out of this life, just as she laboured you in.

An Invisible Papercut

Sienna Scully

I went to wash my hands in the depths of my hometown and discovered I was covered in a million, tiny, papercuts. Slices on my skin of the hurts of my past, the trauma of my childhood.

The papercuts. I have dived into the depths of my hometown, bathing in the streets, beaches, and cafés that are all too familiar. I feel every single papercut over my body now. They are not invisible anymore. They are splitting wider and deeper with each landmark I pass. The house. My house. My home. But it's not my house anymore. Where is my home? This is not just a papercut but a knife that is wedged into my heart. Stabbed into the thumping, blood-filled organ with a cancer diagnosis, wedged further with a death. Twisted with each photograph seen, or memory remembered, or memory that could have been... A knife that I stitched into place as I boarded a plane to the other side of the world. As far away from memories as possible. However, the mind still remembered. The stitches tried to undo themselves when roommates facetimed their mothers, with each birthday that passed, with each 'A' earned, with each tear shed. However, I grabbed my needle and I sewed the knife tighter and tighter, suppressing the pain that came with living life without a mum. A new school, a new state, a new challenge. Run and sew, run and sew, RUN AND SEW.

The pain cannot catch up with me. I will outrun it to the ends of the earth. But then, graduation came. A visa ending... Pandemic. I can keep running for a while longer...

Borders re-opening. Flights re-instating. Overstayed visas expiring. There's a difference now though. I am ready. Healing has been done. Time has passed. I am ready. I exit a plane into the place that birthed and raised me. Excited for nostalgia and connection.

Ping.

What is that?

Ping.

It happened again.

I feel it inside of me. Something is happening. Each stitch is tearing apart more rapidly than I can hold. I am in the depths of it. There is nowhere to run. There is no needle to sew with. The knife has ripped free and is wreaking havoc of my torn and shredded core. Every memory another tear. Every friend's phone call with their mum another slit. Every lost moment and overwhelming sense of needing your mum another gash ripped open. My house. It is not my house anymore. It hasn't been since I was fifteen years old. Where is my home?

An invisible papercut. Not so invisible anymore. There needs to be a caution sign like those at the beach. But instead of 'Beware of Rocks' it will read:

'Beware of bathing in the depths of a place known as home. Unforeseen pain ahead'.

you knew the science of dew

Gina Mercer

a stroke cuts you off
from words
from telling
your bright morning thoughts

then you are gone
                    released

the seagulls continue their daily commute
upriver to the council tip
the seagulls persist

                    but not you, not this time—

today i'm treading the soft dawn grass you walked

could you remind me again   of the science of dew?

Seasons

Brian Purcell

These are no good!
I've unwrapped the new
scissors and taken his hand
but the nails are splitting

curving, horny and yellow
and slip away when I apply
the slightest pressure to cut—
or sometimes just crumble

into dust. In the last days
I've found everything he wanted:
the mobility chair
he can no longer slide into

the walker that stands
expectantly in the corner.
I've shopped for fine chocolates
wafers, prawns, newspapers

the sweet valencias he dreams of—
so hard to find, out of season
he jokes it's a reason to disinherit me.

Yet I try again
and pare each cuticle
slowly, piece by piece.
Ah that's a bit better.

Now he realises
the only victories
are small and temporary
and I breathe freely again

yet I know that, like this
like everything else in his life
next time I visit
the scissors will be lost

yet his nails will keep growing
like ripening valencias.
Soon he will rise from the sheets
into a sweeter light.

Visiting Pop

Beth Clapton

Pop jolts awake, demands to know my name
scowls and says I wear his mother's face
scours his memory trying to place the blame
I fold him in a clumsy half embrace

He scowls and says I wear his mother's face
someone in a room nearby is crying
he recoils from my clumsy half embrace
the cactus on his window ledge is dying

Someone in a nearby room is crying
the clock hands click and jerk but gain no ground
the cactus on his window ledge is dying
he claims his family never comes around

The clock hands click and jerk but gain no ground
Sky News cruels his night and blues his day
he claims his family never comes around
the cold room reeks of Dettol and decay

Sky News cruels his night and blues his day
he scours his memory trying to place the blame
the cold room reeks of Dettol and decay
Pop jolts awake, demands to know my name

Promise

Renee Pettitt-Schipp

This morning the rain fell through the trees
like forgiveness
like everything could be undone,
days of drought had never come
the cat, the fox, the fire, the saw, the salt
as though reaching trees were left
to learn their leaves
the warbler to weave her nest
of webs and bark   suspending her art
                                        in air

I write this poem for you like a prayer
I write with ink of fur and scales singed
for the Carnaby's nest and her rare two eggs
held deep in a hollow before it falls.

All my body knows about you is love
my hidden eggs and the one life fed
is the will of the world expressed
in the shifts of your
unfolding self

today   gazing out of a slow bus window
at the smooth grey back of the river
bright cranes bowing to boats anchored in port

eyes glaze   your gaze is not with the ships
or the water   the weight of books in your bag
a new kind of anchor   like a promise that is hard
to believe

Grieving Artist

Rebekah Lambert

'Write your grief,' they say,
'Get it out of you, every last little bit!'
As though grief's tank doesn't refill,
As though there is an end to this.
'Make art from the heart!' they cry,
'Which part?' I ask, fragmented.
They point to easels, paints and canvas
not realising what I'm lamenting.
'Sing your way through it,' they counsel
'Let the sound fill you with breath.'
But I'm the aching, songless bird,
Gasping with death on my chest.

After the Funeral

Rachel Paxton-Hall

This loss is
bloated, obese
a taut balloon that
begs release
from the pressure but

they took away my sharps
and they cut my nails and
they give me cream
for the stretch marks

how do I get used to
this obesity of grief
around my heart?

It is metastatic, they say
just like mum
but this won't kill me, they say
nor will it be cured

you will feel it in your breath,
your hair, your legs when you walk

I am heavy

my feet sink
the grey carpet is quicksand
and I am buried
like mum, only
I still have a heartbeat.

Rubble

Richenda Rudman

Here, the buildings are shredded,
like skulls with the last remaining flesh.
A wall is gone to show a room inside—
a bowl of lemons on a bisected table,
and sheet music open to a song.

Outside are tongues of flame
and flattened grey slabs
stacked like pancakes.

In the middle, a man covered in grey dust
crouches, holding his daughter's hand.
In high vis, he stares straight ahead
unblinkingly, matching the girl's stillness.

He holds her hand patiently,
as he once did when the street was a street
and she baulked at big dogs.

He tells himself she was sleeping,
wrapped in her soft pink blanket,
which, by some futile miracle,
remains untorn, unmarked.

He berates himself
for not having been there,
for being neither armour nor sword as her oyster world cracked.

A father holds his daughter's hand,
remembering the sweet starfish of it:
how it unfurled, how it gripped
sure, steadfast.

A man approaches the father in the rubble,
pressing water to his lips.
There is nothing to say that will move the man:
the rubble will remain
as long as it does.

Ester Bot Ecocide

Maria Koukouvas (Vouis)

When the clockwork of the planet winds backward

what will happen to vanilla

the orchid's lance withered, my ice-cream will be perfumed

by Ester the smell-bot

and like an earworm pop song

with only three chords

the jazz of real scent will fall mute

cinammon

cardamom

the dying comet star anise

inventory of lost-tongue love

rose oil, prayer of wrist and heart

will be a costly element borrowed by Chanel from the Periodic table,

the catalogue of spent scent

when the Gulf Stream surges anticlockwise

pith of orange

bitter

bitter

bitter

gone.

too young for nutmeg

Veronica Troup

I counted count//—less
bundles of 28 days
webbed consolation
for no overlaps
to cancel you out

I floated sun//—flowers
for your autumn ripped farewell
from a florist
your tiny feet
will never walk into

I welcomed you//—me
to the underworld
to list within moonshine tides
and join my kindred army
of un-living

I felled hope//—ful
you remember more
than unseen un-heldness
fragile fit snug
into the palm
of the nurse's hand

The Perspective Doctor

Robert Edmonds

A doctor with a red nose, a golf green on his head
and a Calvin Klown case by their beds.
What if I kept doing gags and tricks here, all year?
What if I didn't go elsewhere?
What if this was all about you? I won't leave 'til you want me to.
'It's just literally being afraid,' said Robin Williams (not present)
The fearfulness came and took him with it.
Fear confines, restricts, inhibits. But somehow
in Peter, it didn't. And he didn't make quick visits.
He was expansive, expanding the space around him.
He'd head for the Nursing Unit Managers, inevitably
and they'd all have to put their pens down, eventually.
By the time they touched them again, they were different,
they'd expanded and calmed, their edges were softer.
They'd been treated by the perspective doctor
who kept on raising the roof with laughter.
I stood in the beautiful Katoomba Y, all wood and high
ceilings, and called Peter on the phone.
'Am I clowning with you next week?' I asked
'Mate! I'm circling JFK! I don't know how you got through to me!'
It seemed a perfectly natural place for him to be.
'I'm having champagne, I've been bumped up to first class
for helping a man with a racing heart.
Now I'm just kicking back and having a drink.
I've got *hours* before the conference begins!
I'll be back in time for our Monday round
So—where are you calling from? The Y?'
Yes.
I'm calling from the why.
Why can't I cruise that high?
Why can't I take more time, spread more, fear less?
Sure, Peter, you've flown my friend
but you're also raising the roof again

CARRIED

Jennifer Binovec

> 'Some things cannot be fixed; they can only be carried. Grief like yours, love like yours, can only be carried.' Megan Devine

I want you to be able to carry your grief with the lightness of a flower swaying tenderly in the wind. I wish you to blow upon those small, fragile petals and watch as they dance gently in the soft, young breeze. I want you to feel that tranquility as they flutter delicately around you and come to rest slowly upon the earth. I want you to watch these seeds of grief plant themselves again and again, over and over, and I wish you to inhale deeply and breathe in the sweet, beautiful sadness from your overflowing garden of grief.

I wish you to be able to curl up snugly and feel the softness and deep comfort as you rest your weary head upon the pillow of grief. I want you to let those heavy, anguished tears fall and soak into the jagged folds of your sheets of sadness. I want you to pull up the velvet covers and allow the weight of the blanket of sorrow to wrap you in a cocoon of compassion. I want you to whisper quietly into the ear of grief your delicate secrets and your brittle sadness until the faint, early morning light appears.

I want you to be able to thrash, to scream, to yell and to wail, when the journey of grief wrenches you away from the safety of the shoreline, far out into the wild sea, and catches you in a frightening rip of heartache. I want you to shriek that it's not fair. I want you to protest strongly to the dark clouds above. I want you to cry out and scream and howl some more, that horrific nightmare lived over, and then scream again, until your throat is dry and hoarse, ravaged and sore, and your bruised, battered body is submerged by these enormous waves of sorrow.

I want you to exchange your hard-earned knowledge with the people who journey beside you from time to time, weaving your gentle kindness with your thoughts, and I want you to never be ashamed of where you have been, where you are and where you are going. I want your complex narratives to be the exquisitely rich and profound stories that they are.

Grief is so many things. It is yours to hold, to let go of, to cherish, to shrug off, to hug, to cuddle, to comfort, to pierce, to love, to hate, to nurture, to listen to, and to ignore. It is yours to chase after or chase away. It is yours to sing to and to carry upon your shoulders. It is yours to spill from the corners of your eyes. It is yours to share, to curse, to keep secret and hidden, and yours to bury deep down then unearth.

A grief like yours, a love like yours, can only be carried, whichever way you choose.

VISIT

Terry Whitebeach

days are bleak
nights hard wrung
she comes to me
in absence

whispers
Mum Mum
get me out of here
but I cannot

the door is shut
between us
bolted

only in birdsong
may I visit—
in leaf-fall
or rain on thirsty
skin

Cento for a Boy

Sue Aldred

(after Wilfred Owen)

Later, he was brought to me
on a cardboard tray...not fit for purpose.
Waxen, bruised face, small body
wrapped tight in theatre-green cotton.

Transparent lids rested
like veined butterflies, alighted on closed eyes.
Dimpled cheeks, chest unmoving,
lips of saddest blue.

Here was no skin on skin,
no tender first embrace.
No questing mouth to breast
or welcomed cry.

A cold room with no answers.
Night descended outside. Here,
harsh, bright light, illuminating
unutterable grief.

Let us warm him with the sun,
unwrap him to the air, no—
darkness has come.
Show him to the stars
above, in velvet indigo.

My Father Meets Morpheus

Beth Clapton

My father is a sparrowhawk, hanging in the air
yellowed talons scratch and twitch in my palm
swollen knuckles splay to correct his course.
Bright pinprick eyes roll and track invisible prey
scurrying and cowering in fields below.
He tugs air into his chest, riding gusts and eddies
of ragged breaths, to tuck puffs into what space
remains where dark mass encroaches on pink lung
like a fist of cloud before the sun.

My mother crouched, timid as a fieldmouse
to squint against parallax and meniscus
to measure the balm of his days. Only time
can recall him to our waiting gauntlet.
I hold her gaze. We wait for him to swoop
with bloodied mouth to earth again.

He hurtles past, eyes focused for a moment
as strafed by Luftwaffe he clutches his lover's hand
put out that light!
he cries as he plummets through time.
We tug the curtains tighter while he battles Stukas
breath whistling bombs tumbling from the fighter plane.

He tugs the joysticks of our hands, steering
what memory is left of us away from harm.
Is he heading for the clouds or coming in to land?
He issues commands in languages we do not understand.
Across his writhing sheets we wonder
by what right we seek to tether him.
Come back
my mother whispers, but then
let go
Who are we to know he is not king of the skies
defender of the realm
who are we to defined him only
as a mere man sinking
                                        sinking?

Bats

Margaret Aitken

I would see them on the way to work.
Shadowed against the pink-grey sky.
A screaming hurricane of shade,
stripping the highest branches
and replacing the
good leaves with dark snarling fruit
that twitched in the daytime.

They did not come from here.
They chased away the sweet birds
and they shat in the water.
They were   ruinous.
But I liked to watch them on my
way to work   early.

                    This summer
                    they did not
                    return from
                    warmer climates.

I miss watching them.
They are invasive.
They were also here
and alive. Who can
blame tiny creatures
for surviving?   Destructively?

People cheered   when they left
but now   there are no bats
and no sweet birds.

Just   silence.

I moved to a new place and
and there is no greenery
but there are bats,

hanging dead like black fruit on the powerlines.

Till Death Do Us Part

Amy Ocean

Dearly beloved we are gathered here today to mourn the death of me, I hope that's ok
Where shall I Start? Till Death Do us Part.
Death to the parts of me, from the past of me
Rest in peace to the old me who would allow her own needs to recede
Her desires to retire, burned in your fire—her wants left wanton
Rest in peace to the old me who let herself be less-than
Not important, worthless and forgotten. People pleasing, own dreams ceasing
Rest in peace to the old me who was pulled whatever way you needed
Continuously succeeded
The first draft, the stepping-stone, the stopover, but never the home.
Rest in Peace to the old me who sacrificed her parts to make room for us
Infiltrated with the bacteria of betrayal, the amoeba of your weeping
The mitochondria of your hypochondria, the tentacles of your trauma
Rest in Peace to the old me who felt her body was broken—deep hatred unspoken
Patriarchy preaching poison, media manipulating mind to malevolence

Rejecting this magnificence
Rest in Peace to the old me who made excuses—fears limiting her uses
Perfectionism in profuseness
Rest in Peace to the old me who allowed boundaries to be breached
Always within your reach—constant invasion of her space
She's gonna need you to get the hell outa her face
Rest in Peace to the old me who took responsibility for causing temptation
For upsetting the congregation
That her body and how it's adorned could be the cause of your scorn
That she's the reason you have a stumbling block
Instead of you taking control of your own goddam cock.
Now don't think for one second that these deaths were peaceful, pain-free or cruisy
They have been drawn out, confronting and downright confusing.
I thought the pain each time would be the death of me, until I realised it was actually necessary. Severing away those past 'me's'—parts that were preventing me from being free
Evolutionary—ugly crying vulnerability. Revolutionary—broken-hearted bravery
Dearly beloved thank you for gathering today, to delight in my death, my decay, my falling away. So until next time, or till death do us part,
I'll be Resting in my Peace, with a brand-new start.

Glass

Damen O'Brien

I took my mother up the mountain—
there's a glass-making studio there—
she'd been given a lesson for her birthday.

This trip is always bittersweet—
her mother lived there once when
all the shops were farms and forests.

Change, like a betrayal, everywhere—
rainforest hideaways for hippies,
now boutique studios and soap stores.

She looked sadly out of the window—
it's hard to believe your grandmother
ever walked these streets.

On the way down she talked of glas—
to make it, you must blow into a pipe—
a steady breath pushing out a shape

until it cools enough to stay that way.
Every vase is just a cup of someone's air,
lungs composing solid songs from heat.

She left her mistakes snapping in a bin
and the ones she liked, cooling overnight
in the studio oven, to be posted later.

I drove, thinking of perfect forms,
keeping their shapes long after
the woman who breathed them has gone.

Honour the Dark

Autumn Tansey

This is to those who have ever said that the answer is
simple.
That it’s just about changing your mindset.
That it’s about where you are placing your energy.
That life isn’t so hard, it’s that you are making it hard.

To some degree, I agree.
But I also think that’s a load of shit.

Life is not simple.
It is messy and complex,
because we are creatures with a mind that fluctuates
between instinct and consciousness.

Seen in your social media grid, declaring that if you believe enough it will get better than this.
I can't help but wonder, if you,
have ever seen the grandest canyon of grief,
that distant longing between the most terrible lows and the skyward highs that are out of reach.
Because from where I stand, this vast heart contains so much more than simple.

Now don't get me wrong, I do believe in better things to come.
I trust that this will pass,
and that tomorrow is another day.
But today,
as in, right now,
I have to honour the shadows.
Because sometimes we spend longer struggling than we would like.
External circumstances confused with internal truths,
dreaming that life will get better than it is now,
as we hold onto the edges because they give us structure.

My life is not a reflection of what I give my energy to.
Because, I didn't choose to step into the dark.
We don't choose to lose loved ones, to witness injustice, or to feel pain.
We don't choose to invoke a chasm of grief.

So to those that parade as inspiration,
myself included,
telling us that all we have to do is…
Don't forget that,
we *are* already doing our best.
Making it work,
Taking the tiniest steps in whatever direction we can muster,
with vulnerability and grace.

But I will take your suggestion and put it in my pocket for another day.
As a reminder for when I need it most.

My Past Selves and Me

Margaret Leggatt

They're still here. It's getting crowded as the years accumulate.

Usually they're just milling around randomly, although I regularly arrange everybody in order, to make sure nobody's missing. There are a few who might disappear while I'm not paying attention.

1960 tries that, and 1964. They're the ones with things they would like undone. Things that have caused us all a bit of grief. Am I ashamed of those two and others like them? Oh, yes. Sometimes I really do wish they would disappear, but no, I refuse to let them off so easily. When I've got them all lined up, I move in close and look them right in the eye. The spotlight treatment I call it. 'Suffer a little longer,' I say.

Here's the thing, though, if I can digress for a moment. I want to talk about stars, those stars crowding above me when I'm camping, say, on the soft grassy verge of a long, white beach where there's no spotlight, no kind of light, because nobody lives there and the sky's as black as black.

Here's the thing: those stars are probably long gone. Supernova'd or blackholed or whatever process it is that obliterates old stars. Except they haven't gone anywhere, because there they all are, in the sky. I can look right at them.

As I say, getting back to 1960 and '64 and a few other shamefaced selves I haven't mentioned—by all that's logical, by the laws of physics and the passage of time as I understand it, those characters don't exist anymore. But like those stars, they haven't gone away at all; they haven't disappeared into the black hole of history. I can still see them, here in my line-up. I make sure of it.

Who can know for sure if past selves are truly gone, like old stars, extinguished, which in some cases would be a comfort, or if, by being still visible in the dark sky of memory, they remain a real and powerful presence? In either case there's not a lot I can do about it.

So, when I see that sky, those stars, by the beach, those jumbled together points of brightness, here and also not here, I start to think about my past selves, that maybe I could just lie back and look at all of them, at all of us, at all of me.

I could forget the line-ups and the roll checks, the spotlight treatment, the recriminations and regrets. It might be comfortable just being part of this crowd of selves, the commendable ones and the lamentable ones, all smooshed together like the stars. And maybe some will wink out, and some might stick around, or even call out and say, 'Hey, look at me. Don't you forget me.'

And it's all okay. I am the me that's here right now and was before. The same and not the same. Many selves. One self.

HIS THREE FACES

Michael Brown

On the day he died
His life pored over us
His clothes tried us on
His photographs
Watched over us
As he slept like a newborn
Morphine driving him
In an open-top
Through the late afternoon
The sound of each breath
A breaking wave

'That could be you'
My sister says
Holding up another photograph
Of our boy father
His three faces
And two of them now mine
How could I not
Turn back and touch
The fullness
in his hollow cheeks
How could I not greet
the silence
That entered the room
as he left

Fourteen

Helen Goodwin

Fourteen is the year my body is handed over to the collective. Construction workers whistle at me as I walk past each afternoon, oblivious of my school uniform and the innocence of the girl inside it. Or perhaps this titillates them, drunk on the power of being older, stronger and en masse.

Fourteen is the year my parents and I travel overseas, my sister's photo passed around with abandon. Their female friends look at the photo, look up at me, look at the photo, and feel emboldened to comment. They tell me I look *healthier* than my sister as if this is a compliment, but their voices drip with disdain and judgement. For her or for me, I'm not quite sure.

This is the trip that men start paying me attention—over and above my mum. Later, she tells me this is a turning point, when she first notices them noticing *me*. Decades later, she still smarts at the shift, the point at which my presence renders hers invisible.

Fourteen is the year the boys at school call me 'Hot Rod' as I walk past. I might be too nerdy to talk to, but my appearance is ripe for discussion.

And fourteen is the year I start to control my body by controlling my food.

I don't do it consciously, not at first. I start by experimenting with not eating meat. I don't miss it and am proud of my self-discipline. What is initially a one-week experiment with vegetarianism becomes three weeks, then three months, then three years.

My control of *what* I eat soon expands into how *much* I eat. Or how little. I call it a win if I don't eat between breakfast and dinner. Add in a forty-minute walk to school and another forty minutes home, and my body sheds a skin.

And then another.

I eat enough at shared mealtimes to appear normal, and my father is oblivious.

I'm proud that I've become as skinny as my sister, even if it only comes naturally to one of us. Photos reveal sharp elbows and pale skin, almost translucent. My arms cover my concave midriff, as if I'm trying to become smaller still.

Dolly magazine is my monthly bible, so I know about eating disorders from Dolly Doctor. I know anorexia sufferers can develop a soft, downy hair on their backs as their body becomes unable to effectively regulate temperature. This doesn't deter me—instead, it seems something to aspire to.

One night, as I perch on the bathroom bench, I contort my body to get a better view. When I see a soft down on my shoulder blades, I feel elated. Another victory in the battle for control of my body. Me: 1, Public: 0.

Looking back, it hardly seems a coincidence that my eating disorder began when my body became public property. An unconscious attempt to wrest back control of my body for myself.

Unspoken

Elle Searle

Of the two
it was the wrong one who died.
I am left with the lesser and now
I feel contempt.
I am jealous of all those who still have their soul-spirit,
while I must pretend that I am fine.
I invite the guilt to fester and eat my insides
until I feel sick,
to punish myself for thinking these thoughts,
for wishing that this one had died
in place of the other.

A Binary Life

Judi Lane

'When we're gone, we're gone.'

Your breath whispers across my face, melting the end-of-week cobwebs of fatigue.

'Life is binary. We exist. Or we don't. There's nothing in between.'

Provocative. That chocolate velvet voice enticing me with Friday night philosophy.

I uncurl myself from the couch. A rich mouthful of wine kisses my tongue as my tired eyes drink you in. The image of you salves my soul.

We have walked this conversational path before—frequent travellers, neither of us weary, no taint of contempt for the achingly familiar.

I gently counter: 'If life is binary, doesn't that make our existence rather black and white?'

You contemplate, before responding. A ghost of a smile flits across that face, so intimately known that I do not need to touch it to feel its curves and textures. You adore this form of cerebral seduction.

'No, not at all. Think of binary numbers. They have a unique beauty and elegance to their pattern.'

I twirl the remains of dark, red, tears of sticky wine and counter, 'Ah, but isn't the purpose of the binary system to reduce everything to its simplest form? If we live a binary life, doesn't that mean we are stripping it of its textures, its colours, those nuances that make us… us?'

Your eyes shine, amused that I have remembered how to play this verbal game—this delicious dance of wordplay and tease.

'Think about it. Doesn't complexity make everything, *complex*? The circle of life—we're born, we live, we die. Simple. There is nothing more.' You say this with frustrating assuredness, with that trademark confidence in your ability to scientifically analyse and draw laser-like conclusions. Like the binary system, breaking it down to its most uncomplicated form. You just know.

I want to say there is so much more. There is everything in between, everything before and after. It's those non-binary threads that keep us connected.

I gaze intently into those blue eyes, willing you to understand. I will never abandon the tissue-thin fragment of hope that one day, you might see and agree.

We have been having this conversation for six years—ever since you passed away.

Ga-laam (The Crab Dance)

Lakshmi Kanchi

We speak, you and I. The glint
of a moon-soaked, muddy
crustacean in your seaworn eyes.
Its scrape-on-sand sideways
                                        movement
raspy in your voice. Its imagined
chelipeds   wrapped around
your lungs, punctuating silence.

A flaring
that filled seven years of
our lives with needless worry.
Death did come in the end, a slow
crab-shaped   shadow dance.

I watched
it emerge—*zoea*, a pinprick,
from under the seafloor
        of your drowning.
I watched
it pinch at the growing hollow
mapped on your body, the crab-eaten
                                foam of your lungs.
I watched
you turn, bold against the *blue manna*,
swim swim swim seaward, breathless
                        against a wall of wind.

We arrive at this point—time and
time again. Undeterred, I visit its precipice
each night in my dreams. Dreamscapes
change slowly and I watch as the crab
outlives you   in every version
our story tells itself   to me.

'I do not have to enter the land of everlasting sorrow'

Marjorie Lewis-Jones

What's not so clear before you get here is how the losses accumulate, one blow after another, one disease after another, one death after another, loved ones falling from the sky, bad news landing on your back / recently someone told me they'd lost twenty-nine people in a year and I wonder how any of us can cope with that level of subtraction, one star after another, one fairy light after another, fading and winking out / and I do recall my father once telling me that most of his friends were either too sick or too frail to socialise or had died, and I think this was when he was in his late eighties, and while I'm a lot younger than that now, and while not *so many* of my people are dead, some are definitely on struggle street, including my second cousin who got multiple stress fractures in her leg from strolling up a hill and pottering around town with undiagnosed osteoporosis and then slumped in pain in a wheelchair for six weeks and is now walking as if every surface is made of glass / another cousin is slowing down with Parkinson's Disease, falling and hallucinating, troubling the neighbours and the sheep on her property, and yet another is in agony and needs a shoulder reconstruction, this same cousin also has a husband with dementia and the guilt of placing him in a care facility is eating her up, even though it had become impossible for her to keep caring for him at home, she tells me, 'He would escape'/ and, you know, I'm trying to reframe my brain, my heart, my lungs to slide over these slippery surfaces to leap and land as lightly as possible, pushing the pain through the blades, carving up the rink, gripping the little shreds of joy in my fists as I head for the spin so I don't lose myself again in a blizzard of grief.

*The title of this work is taken from the poem 'You're the Top' by Ellen Bass

Welcome

Alyshia Barnes

There's a pineapple on the mantle in the front room of my house. It's the first thing you see when you walk in through the door. I like to sit at the big wooden table and watch the pineapple. I watch it as I eat my breakfast. I've eaten every crumb of toast from my plate, but I haven't touched the milk.

The pineapple hides part of the painting sitting behind it. I had it framed because it's a very special painting. I made it myself. It's of my grandmother dying. I stood over her bed, watching her grey, slackening skin, her teeth yawning inside her spasming jaw as the breath left her lungs in a lurch. The pineapple covers where the catheter enters her hand. She looks less like she's screaming now, and more like she's about to swallow the pineapple whole.

I would never eat the pineapple, but I like to imagine how it would taste. I could cut it in half and eat its insides with an ice cream spoon. Out on the veranda, in my shorts and thongs, juice running through my teeth as I watch people on bicycles and people in cars and bicycles in cars and cars on people. I could eat a spoonful every day. A spoon for every meal. Put it in the blender and drink it instead of milk.

A pineapple smoothie would be yellow. Yellow like chalk before you use it. Yellow like popcorn with too much butter on it. Yellow like cat piss. The smoothie I made this morning was the same colour as my skin and I don't know whether God is calling me fruity or if I want to be mangled in a blender.

The pineapple is starting to melt over the mantle. It's old now. The green is going brown and the yellow is going orange and it's spilling down over the painted wood and dripping into the fireplace. The fire sizzles and the smell is so delicious.

I kick the mantle so hard the wood splinters. I kick it again and my foot breaks through the bricks into the chimney stack. Debris scratches my leg as I pull it loose and blood drips into the fizzing pineapple. I pick it up in fistfuls and shovel it into my mouth. I taste the rot and feel the worms wriggling inside it and me. I throw up so hard it comes out my nose but I keep my mouth shut as I chew and chew and chew. I bite through my tongue and marvel at how the flavour profile shifts. I'm crouched over, eating the drippings up off the floor and my hair catches on fire. I burn and the carpet burns and the house burns. I let myself start to drip drip drip next to the pineapple on the ground. I can see Grandma's catheter now. She leans out of the painting and gobbles me up.

When held hostage to cancer

Lakshmi Kanchi

What does it feel like, I wonder, sitting at the edge of the bed, holding on to that brass bell, its pulled metal sound, to call for help? Fingers unsure. The smell of ground-up herbs pressed to your body. A pasty film of green thump and slew against your rotting, rotted spine. A robust woman made sparse as the disease takes hold of you in full. *What does it feel like?* Your face wrinkled like the creases of an old page that can no longer be contained in the book, and so

it falls

and finds ways to

press into itself. Repeatedly.

An origami flower—our fragrant, fragile *Champa*, soaked in unseasonal rain. The blood moon *bindi* on your forehead as you await passage, eclipsed by the glare of a diminished future.

The sodden, wilting *Champa,* consumed by thoughts; worried if people would know where to find—traces of you. Scattered around in this room, in this house, in your garden. Resounding inside the well from which you drew water. A daily chore. The earthen pot turned inside out, bone-dry and witness to your passing.

Language leaves your lips and replaces the hollow of your mouth with soft sounds. Murmurs that reverberate in my head now when I think of you like that, *Ajji. What does it feel like?* The many small deaths that bring you to the edge, leave your body twisted, face contorted in pain. You refuse medication, refuse relief, refuse ... until the final stretch that takes you over the threshold. You are gone, tugged away at long last.
The gentleness with which you succumb to an unreasonable end. The thread of your breath

left tangled inside the room.

Index

www.ingramcontent.com/pod-product-compliance
Lightning Source LLC
Chambersburg PA
CBHW020514120726
47904CB00003B/825